DEATH
IN LITTLE
TOKYO

TO MY ONLINE FRIEND CAROLYN —

HOPE YOU HAVE FUN
WITH THIS — SEE YOU
ON DOROTHL !

BEST,
Dale Furutani

古谷

To my online Tilton family,

Hope you have fun
with this — see you
on Danthl!

Best wishes,

古谷

DEATH IN LITTLE TOKYO

A KEN TANAKA MYSTERY

Dale Furutani

ST. MARTIN'S PRESS
NEW YORK

Design by Ellen R. Sasahara

Library of Congress Cataloging-in-Publication Data

Furutani, Dale.
     Death in Little Tokyo : a Ken Tanaka Mystery / by Dale Furutani.
          p.   cm.
     ISBN 0–312–14580–2
     1. Japanese Americans—California—Los Angeles—Fiction.
I. Title.
PS3556.U778D43 1996
813'.54—dc20   96-23192
                                                              CIP

First Edition: October 1996

10 9 8 7 6 5 4 3 2 1

To Sharon for her love.

Kafuku wa azanaeru nawa no gotoshi.

Bad and good are intertwined like rope.

—JAPANESE FOLK SAYING

ACKNOWLEDGMENTS

Thanks to Kayko Matsumoto Sonoda for sharing her camp records with me. Also thanks to Neeti Madan and M.N. for their advice and patience.

DEATH
IN LITTLE
TOKYO

The murder was calculated, cruel, and callous. Horace Peavy was brutally slain and two million dollars in negotiable bonds was stolen. Peavy was first hit on the head with the type of sledgehammer used to stun cows, then his body was taken and fed through a sausage grinder, turning him into breakfast sausage that was sold to a big restaurant chain. It was an effective way to get rid of the corpse, but I may never eat a Grand Slam breakfast again!"

The laughter echoed in the old "Farmer Bob's" meat packing plant. The gaunt rafters of the plant formed a Gothic backdrop to the grisly tale I had to tell. The twelve people sitting before me on folding chairs looked more like an audience than a jury. I looked at their faces and scowled.

"Yes, I know it has its macabre and amusing aspects, especially since Mr. Peavy was, by all accounts, known as a pig." More snickers. "But, ladies and gentlemen, this is hardly an amusing matter, even though one of you has suggested that Mr. Peavy should have been marketed as turkey sausage instead of pork sausage." More laughter.

"In my experience a murder as brutal as this one can only have two causes. The first is the killer is mentally deranged; a psychopath or sociopath with little or no regard for human suffering or human life. Unfortunately, the front pages of our newspapers present us with increasing evidence that this type of killer is active in our society.

"The other type of killer is someone who has nursed a grudge for years or even decades. To motivate an otherwise normal person to kill in a frenzied and brutal manner requires an overwhelmingly powerful motivation. A motivation built up over time and tied to deep feelings of self-worth and being wronged. A motivation that requires more than the simple act of murder when the deed is finally done. A motivation that requires slaughter.

"In this group there is no evidence that anyone fits the profile of a casual killer, so I knew I was searching for someone who had quelled his or her rage for years, until that rage could only be quenched by feeding Peavy, piece by piece, into the sausage grinder. The bizarre demise of Mr. Peavy and the disposal of his body provided the first clue that allowed me to unravel this case. It started me on the trail of evidence that allows me to prove conclusively which of you killed him." I swept my finger in a grand arc, pointing at all the people gathered before me. Some of the faces showed anticipation. A few, including Mary Maloney, who knew the murderer, showed a knowing smirk.

"I think it's appropriate that we're meeting in this old meat packing plant for the conclusion of this mystery. You see, not only was the murder perpetrated in this plant, but it was in this plant that the motivation for murder was born." I gave each of the people on the panel a hard stare. Mary Maloney was now grinning openly at my theatrics.

"Mr. Peavy was not the best example of enlightened manhood, and several of you suffered from his cruel taunts and crude sexual advances. His long-suffering wife, Agnes, could have killed him for his many infidelities. But she had no opportunity to know about the two million dollars in negotiable bonds that were stolen when Peavy was killed because Mr. Peavy kept her isolated from his business affairs." I looked at a woman wearing a dowdy dress and a mousy brown wig.

"His business partner, Harvey Goodfellow, has been acting suspiciously recently. But Goodfellow is known as a man of infinite patience and legendary goodwill. That's the only way he could continue with Peavy as a business partner for all these years. It seemed strange that some recent change could result in a murder as brutal as this one, and in fact his furtiveness was simply an attempt to cover up an affair between him and the head bookkeeper of the plant, Penny Inkcolumns." The two star-crossed lovers looked at each other from where they sat at opposite ends of the twelve-person panel.

"All of the rest of you had good reason to kill Mr. Peavy, but only one of you had to endure his crude advances eight hours a day, five days a week, for almost five years. Only one of you knew when the bonds would be in Mr. Peavy's office, and when they would be out of the safe. Only one of you had the ability to lure Mr. Peavy into staying late on that fateful night, on the promise of a long hoped for romantic tryst. Only one of you has the unusual distinction of having graduated from both a secretarial school and a meat cutting school. And only one of you could assure herself that she would never eat the Peavy-tainted sausage, because only one of you is a vegetarian!" Pointing dramatically at a pretty woman in a tight red dress and blond wig, I said, "And that person is Clarissa Shorthand, Mr. Peavy's secretary!"

Clarissa jumped to her feet and shouted, "Yes! Yes, I did it! And you know what? I'm glad! I'm glad I tell you, glad!"

The panel dissolved into laughter.

Mary stood up and said, "Very good. Also very hammy, but since we're in an old meat packing plant, that's probably appropriate." She looked at the rest of the panel. "I think Mr. Tanaka has proven that he has completely unraveled this particular mystery. This was one of the most competitive mysteries we've had in a long time. Both Mr. Tanaka and Mr. Duncan Hathaway submitted their written solutions to the mystery within a few minutes of each other. As you know, our by-laws call for a verbal exposition by all those who solve the mystery at the same time. Mr. Hathaway unraveled who had done the murder and the details of the two million dollars in bonds, but he didn't uncover the nice fact that Ms. Shorthand is a vegetarian, so unless there's an objection from the panel, I'd like to declare Mr. Ken Tanaka the grand prize winner for this month's mystery. All in favor?"

Panel members raised their hands or said "aye." Ezekial Stein, the president of the Los Angeles Mystery Club, just grunted his assent, but that was just Ezekial's way and I took no offense.

"All right," Mary said, "At tonight's banquet at Nicola's restaurant, Ezekial will announce that Ken is the grand prize winner. By the way, if all of you don't know it yet, Ken will also be setting up next month's mystery, and since we've got him here maybe we can coax him into giving us a little preview of what we have in store next month."

"Shouldn't I save it for the banquet?" I asked.

"After the shameless performance we've seen here this afternoon, I don't think there will be any problems with getting you to repeat what you tell us for a much larger audience at the banquet," Mary said grinning.

"Well, first let me thank you for awarding me the grand prize. It's my first, and that Silver Dagger will mean a lot to me when I finally get my hands on it this evening." The panel applauded and I actually felt myself blushing. After two years of trying, this was the first time I had beaten the other players at solving the mystery. Of course, it helped that Mary Maloney was involved in running this month's mystery and thus was unable to compete for the top prize. Mary had won more than her share of prizes for being the one to unravel the club's monthly mysteries. But regardless of that, it still felt awfully good.

"Next, I want to thank Mary and Bob LaBossiere for organizing this weekend's mystery." I gave Mary and Bob, who had played Harvey Goodfellow, a round of applause, and the rest of the panel joined in.

"Finally, I want to tell you that if you loved the *Maltese Falcon,* you will love the mystery I intend to put together. It will be set in Los Angeles's Little Tokyo district, which isn't too far from here, and it will involve the rare and fabled Jade Penguin. You will learn about the exotic history of this fabulous statue and make your way through some of the locations in Little Tokyo as you try to uncover the secret of this priceless artifact. I won't be able to wrangle as impressive a setting as this meat plant," I waved a hand around me, "but I think you'll have fun. Next month's mystery will be the first time I've put together a whole club mystery on my own so I hope my winning the grand prize this time out is a good omen for next month!"

I sat down with what I hoped was a suitably modest expression on my face and Mary concluded the meeting. Several members of the panel came over to congratulate me on my win as Mary left the room to inform Duncan that he came in second.

After thanking the panel members I left and saw Mariko waiting in the meat plant's lobby, sitting on a folding chair. When she saw me she raised an eyebrow and I gave her a thumb's up.

"So you did it," she said.

"Yep, they'll announce it at the banquet tonight. They had to have a tie-breaking session because Duncan Hathaway turned in his written solution within fifteen minutes of me, but I found more of the clues than him and they gave me the grand prize."

"Isn't Duncan the weird guy who runs around in the Sherlock Holmes outfit?"

I laughed. "There're actually a couple of members who dress up like their favorite fictional detectives. But yes, Duncan is one who dresses up for the mysteries."

Mariko shook her head. "You guys take this mystery stuff too seriously."

"It's just good fun. Besides, you must take it pretty seriously yourself, because you're going to help me with next month's mystery."

"Hey, I've got to support you in your endeavors no matter how nutty they get."

I've never thought of the activities of the Los Angeles Mystery Club as exactly nutty, but maybe that was because I was caught up in the nuttiness. Every month the club members pool their money and talents and create a type of living theater: a murder mystery acted out during the course of a Saturday. The club members either try to solve the mystery or play parts in the drama. The idea is to figure out 'who dunnit' before the awards banquet that night. Everyone writes down their theory of the crime and the name of the murderer, and the first one with the correct answer gets a trophy. Everyone who solves the mystery, no matter if they were first or not, also gets a certificate. It's a silly pastime for adults, but fun.

I actually met Mariko through the club. As an aspiring actress, she had been hired to play an exotic femme fatale for one of the mysteries. I found her both femme enough and fatale enough to do something completely uncharacteristic for me: I pursued her. To my surprise, we hit it off and we had been an item for about six months, long enough for us to drop most of our pretenses and to start acting like ourselves. That's when things get both serious and dangerous.

But at this moment I wasn't thinking serious or dangerous thoughts. I was trying to decide where I was going to display my Silver Dagger trophy in my apartment.

A couple of weeks later I was involved in another murder. Well, I guess to be accurate, I should say I was planning a murder.

"Lissen, sweetheart," I said in a passable Bogart imitation. "If you want anything, just whistle. You know how to whistle, don't you? Just put your two lips together and blow." Wait a minute. That was Lauren Bacall's line.

I sighed because I couldn't recall what Bogart's line was. It didn't matter anyway. Let's face it, physically I couldn't muster the mass to imitate Bogart's tough presence. I preferred Alan Ladd when playing a detective. The compact Ladd was much more my size.

I looked at myself in the large mirror I had propped up against the wall and decided I still cut a pretty dashing figure. I figured I looked like a worthy recipient of the Silver Dagger trophy for unraveling the L.A. Mystery Club's phony murder.

I was dressed in a tan trench coat and a gray hat. The props helped to compensate for my small frame and delicate features . . . two curses for someone who secretly aspired to be a 1930s hard-boiled detective. Of course, my being a Japanese-American from Hawaii is also an impediment to this aspiration. The only Asian detectives I remember from old movies were Warner Olan doing his Charlie Chan bit or Peter Lorre doing an incredibly campy Mister Moto. At least Charlie Chan was from Honolulu, although nobody I've ever met from Hawaii actually looked and talked like Warner Olan did.

My face is round with a slightly squared jaw. My eyes are more deeply set than the Asian stereotype, but many Asians, particularly in Japan or Southeast Asia, have deep set eyes. I have the epicanthic fold that characterizes Asians everywhere, and of course my eye color is deep brown and I have black hair.

The tan Burberry trench coat was a good fit, but somehow the felt fedora just didn't look right. I pulled it low over my eyes, but that just blocked my vision. I pulled it off and tried placing it on my head at a rakish angle, but a shock of black hair peeked out and the effect was just goofy. I put it squarely on my head and tried bending down the brim a little. Then I sighed. It wasn't perfect, but it was the best of all the variations I had tried. I guess I just wasn't used to seeing myself in a hat.

I walked over and took off the trench coat. It was a hot August in Los Angeles, and hats and trench coats were definitely not the attire that suited the weather, especially in an old office building with marginal air-conditioning. I hung the trench coat on the old clothes rack that stood in the corner of the office and surveyed my temporary kingdom.

A large wooden desk with many dings and dents dominated the room. Old oak file cabinets stood against the wall next to the propped-up mirror. Four pictures were hung on the walls: photos of Bogart, Alan Ladd, and Cagney, plus a poster for *The Maltese Falcon*. The next wall had two windows that looked down on Second Street. In reverse order, I could see the back of gilt letters that said KENDO DETECTIVE AGENCY—KEN TANAKA, DET. on both windows. The letters were the most expensive things in the room.

The furniture was all borrowed or rented. My girlfriend Mariko Kosaka had supplied most of it through one of the little theater groups she belonged to. Theater props were most appropriate because I was setting up a murder as theater.

I'd gone all out for the mystery I was creating. Besides renting a cheap office in Little Tokyo, I had business cards printed up, installed a phone, and had the proper signs put up in the lobby and on the windows.

My plan was to have the members of the mystery club come to the office to kick off the mystery. The office would act as sort of a hub to the action, and members of the club would have to go to various parts of Little Tokyo to unearth clues.

I had bought several props with a Japanese motif, and was in the midst of evolving a complicated mystery involving a stolen jade statue of supposedly priceless value (the Jade Penguin), a variety of cryptic clues scattered around Little Tokyo, and (of course) a couple of murders. Some members of the club would play the parts of villains or stooges, and the other members of the club would be expected to follow the trail of clues to unravel the puzzle and solve the "crime."

Usually these things were put together by a committee, but except for Mariko's help I had put this one together pretty much on my own. I'd noticed that the mysteries put together by committees were prone to leaks as members of the committee couldn't resist dropping cryptic hints to friends. It was as bad as Congress or some other notorious gathering of blabbermouths.

Doing things on my own precluded the chance for leaks, but it meant endless hours putting things together for the mystery to come off right. That meant either a compulsive personality or a lot of time on my hands. I confess to being doubly guilty.

Like many in America, I found myself starting over while on the other side of forty. A failed marriage, a frustrating job and a pink slip as part of the process euphemistically known as "corporate downsizing" had all added up to plenty of time to plan fake murder mysteries. Mariko had given me as much help as possible, but between work, little theater, and AA meetings, she really didn't have much time to put into the effort.

I stepped away from the clothes rack and took the hat off. With the flick of a wrist, I sent it sailing toward the hat rack. At the last second the unruly swatch of felt veered to one side and fell to the floor, refusing to hang itself on the coat rack peg I was aiming for. Thinking the hat was an apt metaphor for the way my life was going, I walked over and hung it on the rack.

I sat down behind the desk and placed a paper sack before me. I reached in, took out a pair of disposable chopsticks, and split them in two with a practiced hand. In good Japanese restaurants they give you polished disposable chopsticks, and you don't have to rub them together to get rid of the small splinters. You're supposed to know the difference, and not automatically rub chopsticks together. After glancing at these chopsticks, I rubbed them together vigorously.

I took a plate out of the sack and looked at it. Staring up at me was an assortment of sushi. The small mounds of rice were covered with raw fish, encircled by pieces of flavored seaweed. A tiny clump of pink ginger and a dab of green *wasabi* (horseradish) completed the plate.

I glanced at my watch and noted that it was only 10:15 in the morning. Somehow knowing that it was that early made me slightly queasy about the sushi.

The idea seemed a bit bizarre, but it had some sense to it. In order to attract some early morning clientele, the Oshima Sushi bar ran a special. If you came in before 10 A.M., you got a full sushi plate for just four dollars. A sushi brunch seemed like an ideal combination of delight and economy. But staring at the limp, red slices of raw tuna, I decided I'd just as soon have a ham omelet.

Maybe it was just the idea of sushi for breakfast that gave me a problem. If I actually started eating, I might enjoy myself. So I opened a plastic pouch of soy sauce, poured it into a small plastic cup, and took a dab of wasabi off the plate and put it into the sauce, mixing it in. Bracing myself, I picked up a piece of sushi with my *hashi* (chopsticks) and dipped it into the small container of sauce.

I had the sushi halfway to my mouth when I noticed a visitor had opened the office door and was standing tentatively at the threshold.

She was dressed simply in a white suit that showed her tan to good advantage. Under her arm she had a black purse. I'm not an expert at such things but I figure it costs a lot of money to dress so plainly but look so good, and the dress, purse, and shoes all looked expensive. Very expensive.

She was about five foot ten and her blonde hair was carefully coifed in the windblown style that looks so terrible when it really gets windblown. Her eyes were a very clear gray that stared at me with quizzical appraisal. I put down the piece of sushi.

She walked up to the desk and said, "Mr. Tanaka?" Her voice was well modulated and soft. It was hard to tell her age. I'd say late twenties, but someone so well groomed and made up could easily be ten or fifteen years older. Maybe even older with a good facelift.

"Yes."

"Kendo Detective Agency?"

My brain started racing. The classic start for a mystery story: pretty woman walks into detective's office looking for help. I immediately thought this has to be a setup. Some other member of the mystery club hired this blonde to show up at the office to get a mystery within a mystery going before I could get my own stumper launched. I had told them that my mystery was loosely based on *The Maltese Falcon*, and now someone was playing out the opening.

Not many members of the club knew about the office yet, and only Mariko knew the address. Mariko. Maybe Mariko had gotten an actress friend to come down to start her own mystery going as a challenge? Looking at the woman, I thought she was certainly pretty enough to be an actress. I decided to play along.

"That's right. Can I help you?"

"Perhaps you can. I do need some help. Can we talk now? I wouldn't want to disturb your meal." The tone of her voice, however, clearly indicated that it wouldn't bother her to do just that.

"It's no disturbance," I said, putting down the hashi. "I was done anyway. It would take another couple of hours before I'd really find this appetizing. Please sit down," I said, indicating one of the chairs in the office. She settled into a chair with a dancer's grace, like a falling apple blossom. "Could you tell me your name?"

"My name is Rita Newly."

I half expected Wonderly, Mary Astor's name in the *Maltese Falcon*, but since this was a new mystery I guess New-ly was also appropriate.

"How did you find out about me, Ms. Newly?"

"Actually, I saw your name on the window as I drove by. I stopped on an impulse because I need some help." She seemed composed, but her hands nervously grasped at her purse. Mariko had once told me some auditions were hard because the hardest performance to give is in front of just one person. I tried to look sympathetic to put her at ease.

"I've never dealt with a private detective before," she said, "so perhaps you can answer some questions for me before I get into details."

I gave her my warmest smile. Part of the smile was because I was starting to get into the situation, wondering what Mariko had come up with. Part of the smile was because, looking at her, it just wasn't hard to do. "Sure, I'll answer any questions I can."

"First, is our discussion confidential?"

"Absolutely."

"And you'll maintain that confidentiality?"

"As long as I'm not asked to do anything illegal," I said, in the most professional manner I could muster.

"Good," she said. "Then maybe you can help me."

"What is it you'd like me to do?"

"I want you to pick up a package."

I was surprised. "Is that all?"

"That's right. I'll pay you five hundred dollars to do it."

I could almost feel my eyes brighten at the mention of the fee. No one would pay $500 for a simple errand, so the plot was bound to thicken soon.

"Just what kind of package do you want me to pick up?"

"It's rather personal."

Finally things would start to get complicated. I leaned forward in my seat. I was well and truly hooked, already into the fun and wanting to play along. "Look, I'll do it for you," I said. "But I want to assure myself that I'm not getting involved with something that's illegal. To do that, I really have to know what I'm picking up."

"Well," Rita started. She hesitated and looked down, then she looked up at me. Her eyes had a wetness hinting of tears. A few moments before she had seemed so confident and in control of herself. I was surprised by the sudden transformation. There's nothing as appealing to most men as a pretty woman who needs help. Although I knew that intellectually, I still felt a small part of my heart melt. This woman was good.

"Please tell me, Ms. Newly," I said gently. "Maybe I can help." Despite the apparent breakdown in her composure, I found one trait of Rita's very disquieting. Her eyes didn't seem to blink much. Despite the dramatic pause, the looking down, and the hint of tears, when her eyes moved back up to look into mine, they were as wide and clear as when she first walked into the office. They were the eyes of a cobra fixed on a mouse.

"The package contains some pictures. They're pictures of me." Her voice was very quiet, and I had to strain to hear the last sentence.

"What kind of pictures?"

"Well, it's very embarrassing," she said. "And kind of a long story."

I shrugged. "Why don't you tell it to me? I'm not trying to embarrass you, but you have to understand I need to know what I'm getting involved in."

"I'm a singer and a dancer," Rita started. That didn't surprise me. "About six months ago, I saw an advertisement looking for singers and dancers to go to Japan. The salary was very good, and it involved free travel in the Orient. The only hitch was you had to agree to a one-year contract. At the time I was single and I didn't have a steady boyfriend, so I decided to audition. I got the job. They sent me to Japan, but when I got there I discovered they had a quite different type of entertainment in mind. It turned out they were recruiting singers and dancers, but they also wanted us to be . . ." Her voice trailed off.

I figured what was coming, but I coaxed anyway. "Yes?"

"They wanted us to be part-time prostitutes."

"I've heard about that sort of thing." So had Mariko, I thought.

"Well, it's true," Rita said. "I refused go along with it. I made it plain that I was hired as a singer and a dancer, not as a whore." She spat out the word. "They made it very hard for me to keep saying no to them. They never used force or anything, but there was constant pressure to entertain guests after the show and to do the things they wanted me to. Anyway, I got tired of it, but I was stuck in a foreign country and didn't have enough money to get back home."

I nodded sympathetically, encouraging her to go on.

"Since I wouldn't go along with them on the prostitution, they said they would tear up the contract and give me enough money to get home if I did some nude modeling for them. I've done lingerie modeling, and I figured it wasn't that much different. Besides, it would get me home. So I said okay."

"And . . ."

"And I posed for them. They wanted me to get in some strange poses, but at the time I didn't think much about it. They kept their word about paying me enough to get back to the States and they even tore up my contract."

"So what does this have to do with the package you want me to pick up?"

"Well, about three months ago, right after I got back to the States, I met a nice older gentleman. I won't tell you it was a whirlwind romance, but after my experience in Japan, some stability and financial security looked good. Maybe safety was what I was really looking for. Anyway, we've decided to get married. About a week ago I got some photographs in the mail."

"The photographs you posed for?"

"Yes, but they were different. Somehow they managed to alter the photographs so it looked like I was doing things quite different from just posing nude."

"Such as?"

"They managed to add men and even a dog to the photographs. It was disgusting. If my fiancée saw them, I'm sure it would ruin my chances of getting married."

"Even if you explained what happened and that the pictures are altered?"

"He's very conservative," she said. "He doesn't even know I posed for lingerie advertising. He knows I wasn't a virgin when he met me, but he's very possessive. I'm sure he'd call off the marriage if he ever saw those pictures."

"And with the pictures I suppose you got a request for money."

"That's right."

"How much?"

"That doesn't really matter. I've already paid it."

I frowned. I expected a complication where I would get involved in fake ransom drop-offs and a bevy of blackmailers. I was a little disappointed. "That's too bad. My advice is don't pay. Blackmail has the habit of stretching out and never ending. You should call their bluff."

"If they try it again after we're married, I might do that," she said. "But right now I don't want to do anything that might jeopardize my marriage."

"And the package you want me to pick up?" I prompted her.

"Those are the photographs I paid for."

"Are you getting the negatives, too?"

"That's right."

"And when I pick up the package, you want me to make sure you've gotten both the photographs and the negatives."

"No, I don't," she said hastily. "I don't want anyone seeing those photographs. They kept their word about giving me enough money to go home and tearing up my contract. I'm sure they'll keep their word on this, too."

"But they double-crossed you over what they did with the pictures."

"We didn't have an agreement on that. I just wasn't bright enough to think of all the possibilities or the kinds of trouble it might cause me later. I just want you to pick up the package."

"And who has this package?"

"A man named Susumu Matsuda. He's staying at the Golden Cherry Blossom Hotel. He's here from Japan. Anyway, I've already arranged for him to hand over the package. But I don't want to go over and meet him to pick it up. Frankly, I'm a little scared."

I nodded sympathetically. "And after I pick up the package?"

"I want you to hold the package until I call for it. If you can arrange to pick it up today, I'll call you tomorrow."

"All right," I said. "Mr. Susumu Matsuda at the Golden Cherry Blossom." I made a quick note on a piece of paper.

Rita opened her purse, took out a Gucci wallet, and pulled out some bills. "Here's a deposit. I'll give you the balance after you've picked up the photographs. Is that satisfactory?"

"Most satisfactory." I stuffed the bills into my pocket without looking at them.

"Can I have one of your cards, so I'll know what phone number to call?" I was now sure this was a game set up by Mariko. Only Mariko knew I had a phone installed in the office and fake business cards printed up.

"Certainly," I fumbled in the top drawer of the desk and pulled out one of the fake cards.

Rita looked at the business card. "Okay, Mr. Tanaka. I'll be counting on you."

"I'll do my best, Ms. Newly."

I escorted her to the door of the office and watched her as she walked down the hall toward the creaky elevator. Before she turned the corner to the elevator she looked back at me, as if she expected me to be there. I smiled and tried to wave reassuringly. She smiled back and turned the corner.

When I returned to the office I closed the door and started laughing. I was convinced that Mariko was the mastermind behind the little charade I had just gone through. I reached into my pocket and pulled out the small wad of bills. The laughter died. I was expecting stage money, but there in the palm of my hand were three crisp one hundred dollar bills.

Mariko was the proverbial struggling actress. For her to put up three hundred dollars for a joke was, in itself, a joke. I decided to talk to her.

Mariko disdained the standard actor's job as a waitress and she worked at a dress boutique in Little Tokyo. It was only a few blocks from the rented detective office, so I committed what passes for a peccadillo in Los Angeles and walked. The Kawashiri Boutique is part of a tourist complex on First Street known as Japanese Village. It was designed by a Korean, so it looks like a Korean's version of what a Japanese Village in Los Angeles should look like. That's America.

The entrance to Japanese Village is marked by a three-story *yagura,* or fire tower. A *yagura* was used in ancient Japan as a watchtower to look for the incipient signs of smoke in crowded cities. The *yagura* in L.A. is made from bolted together telephone poles, so it would hardly qualify as a museum piece, but I suppose it could be used to spot a tourist bus and the incipient signs of cash.

A cluster of new buildings radiate out from the tower: numerous restaurants, gift shops, bakeries, toy stores, souvenir shops, and a couple of dress shops, including the Kawashiri Boutique. As I walked in, Mariko was helping a couple of customers.

Mariko had on a simple navy dress with a colorful red and gold scarf draped over her shoulder. She's only five feet three inches tall, but that isn't a particular handicap in a shop that caters to older

Japanese women. It is a handicap in her acting.

Her face is round with a small pointed chin. She has a cute button nose and wide brown eyes. Japanese faces have a wide variety of types (at least to other Japanese). Mrs. Kawashiri, who owned the boutique, has a broad flat face that wouldn't look out of place on a Korean, Mongol or Eskimo. Mariko has the same kind of features as me, which look more Southeast Asian.

Mariko's black hair is shoulder length, and she usually wears it with a sweeping lock across her forehead. Her smile has a special magic for me. Her even white teeth give mute testament to the wisdom of her parent's investment in braces when she was a kid. (She told me once how she hated the braces. Selfishly I thought only of the results instead of the process.)

Her figure is trim, but with a nice swell to her hips and beautifully straight legs, not the *daikon* legs that so many Japanese women complain about. *Daikon* is a large, long, and lumpy white radish used in Japanese cooking, and the comparison of legs to radishes is not a flattering one.

I'm forty-two. Mariko is in her mid-thirties, and like me she's had a failed marriage. Also like me, her first marriage was to a Caucasian. That's a topic we've talked about many times with no good resolution.

At the time of her divorce, Mariko was both an alcoholic and working as a loan officer in a bank. I don't know if the two were related. When she hit thirty she decided life was too short to continue working for the green eyeshade crowd. She also decided that her drinking was controlling her, not vice versa. She started alternately attending Alcoholics Anonymous meetings and taking acting lessons. When she worked up the courage, she quit her job and started acting full-time. She also got a divorce from her husband.

She told me she was pretty miserable when she first split up with her husband, but not miserable enough to get back with him. She said he's an alcoholic, too, although he hasn't recognized it yet. When they were first married it was fun to party and be drunks together, but as the drinking became more serious it ceased being fun. Since the divorce both her sobriety and acting career have had their ups and downs. She slipped once on her drinking during her first year in AA, but she's been sober for almost four years. She's appeared in several plays and one TV commercial, but she isn't able to make a living just acting so she works at the dress shop.

The owner of the dress shop, Mrs. Kawashiri, is really good about letting Mariko leave for auditions, and it's a comfortable relationship. Besides, Mariko gets her clothes at a discount, although most of her clothes are special orders because Mrs. Kawashiri, who is in her sixties herself, caters to a much older clientele.

When she was able to take a break, Mariko and I went into the boutique's back room and I gave her a quick rundown on my encounter with Rita Newly. "I thought you set up the whole thing as a joke," I said as I finished, "But when she laid these on me," I flashed the three one-hundred-dollar bills, "I thought that something was very wrong."

Looking at the money, Mariko said, "I did set up the whole thing, and I'll thank you to hand over my money." She solemnly extended her hand.

Surprised, and a little hesitant, I almost handed over the cash. I peered at her and said, "Are you teasing me?"

She laughed. "Of course! Do you think I'd hand over three hundred bucks just because I have nothing better to keep me amused? Besides, you seem a little too interested in this woman. You have a thing for blondes."

My ex-wife was a blonde. We were moving into uncomfortable territory. I did what most men try to do in similar circumstances: I changed the subject. "So what do you think I should do about the package?" I said.

Mariko gave me an appraising look. I don't think she was fooled by such an obvious ploy, but she took pity on me and played along. "What do you mean?"

"Well, she's paying me five hundred dollars to pick it up, so I think I should go over and do it. Although I'm still living off my severance pay, the bottom line is that I'm unemployed and I shouldn't look a gift horse in the mouth."

She got serious on me. "Ken, this isn't a gift horse. It's some kind of job. It's nuts for you to go ahead and do it."

"What's so nuts about it?"

"You're not a private eye. Repeat after me: 'I am not a private eye.' You shouldn't go ahead and run her errand. What kind of person would pay that much for an errand, anyway?"

"Are you sure you didn't set the whole thing up?"

She sighed. "Number one, I don't have hundreds of dollars I can use just to play a joke on you. Number two, her story stinks. Number three, her story really, really stinks! I'd be much more clever than that. Do you think she's serious about this picture business?"

"Do you think it's someone in the L.A. Mystery Club setting things up to play a joke on us? You know, sort of a mystery within a mystery."

Mariko shrugged. "You know the other members better than me. But three hundred dollars is a lot to put up. How do they know you won't just spend it and not play along with the gag?"

"It's a puzzle, isn't it?"

"Why don't you try calling her and see if she has any more to say," Mariko suggested.

I looked at Mariko sheepishly. "Well actually I didn't get a phone number or address from her."

"Very astute," Mariko said dryly. "So what are you going to do?"

"I think I'll go and pick up the package."

"What if it's drugs or something?"

"I'll worry about that when I see the package. If it's something like that, I'll just turn it over to the police. It's possible that Rita is telling the truth, and I don't mind picking up five hundred dollars just for being a messenger boy."

"Ken, nobody pays five hundred dollars and goes to a P.I. if they just need a messenger. Messengers cost a lot less than that. Haven't you been listening to me? There's got to be something involved here that we don't understand. I can't believe this. Even though you've got the office and the fancy raincoat, you are not a private investigator. You don't have a P.I.'s license and you haven't been trained. I enjoy participating in the L.A. Mystery Club weekends with you, but those weekends are fantasy, and you shouldn't confuse fantasy with reality. You might get hurt."

"Relax," I said with bravado. "I'm not going to get hurt. I'm just going to act as a messenger boy and collect five hundred bucks for my troubles. Some people in this town have more money than brains. Five hundred bucks to them is like five dollars to you or me." My pride was stung by Mariko's tone and warning. I'm a Vietnam veteran with a bronze star and a purple heart. I was confident of my abilities.

Mariko reached over the table and placed her hand on my arm. It felt small but warm through the sleeve of my shirt. "I'm just worried about you. Please don't be so silly. Let's call the police about this."

"I don't know what I'd be calling them about. Besides, remember, she wants to keep things quiet because she's getting married to some rich guy soon. I think she made a mistake and took me for a real P.I., but for five hundred dollars I'm going to shut up and do what she tells me."

Mariko put her hands to her head in mock frustration. At least I think it was mock. She rolled her eyes to the heavens and said, "Arrrgh!"

"This is not the smoothest time to bring this up," I continued, "but are you going to stop by my place tonight?"

"I'd stop by, but tonight is Thursday. I've got rehearsals."

Mariko was involved with the East West Players theater group in Hollywood. Thursday nights she went to classes and rehearsals. Before class the group met to clean up the theater, build sets, and do other maintenance.

"Can't you skip it tonight?"

"You know I'd like to, but you also know that I'm up for a part and I'm not going to get it without pulling my weight around the theater. That's how little theater works, Ken."

"Okay. But your theatrical ambitions are sure putting a dent in my love life."

"I know it's tough," she said. "But between theater and AA, a good chunk of my life isn't my own. If you really need me to, I could stop by after rehearsal."

I bit my lip and said, "No. Better not. I might be able to arrange to pick up that package tonight. Rita said she wanted me to have it by tomorrow."

Before Mariko could launch into another protest over my picking up the package, Mrs. Kawashiri came into the back room. She was a short, plump woman who still looked stylish. She was a good advertisement for the clothes normally carried in the shop. Her husband was totally incapacitated by a stroke and she needed the shop as much for human contact as for financial support. She sort of adopted the helpers that worked for her in the shop, and she was always very kind to Mariko. Somehow by extension she had adopted me, too. When she saw me, a smile came across her broad face.

"Ken-san," she said. "Seeing Mariko again?"

"He's just here bothering me, Mrs. Kawashiri. I was about to kick him out so I could come help you in the shop," Mariko said.

"Nonsense. You never take your breaks, so you should spend a little time when your boyfriend visits."

"You tell her, Mrs. Kawashiri," I encouraged. "She always ignores me."

"You shouldn't do that," Mrs. Kawashiri said. "Look at him. He looks like he's been losing weight. Have you been eating right, Ken?"

"He didn't eat much of a breakfast today," Mariko said. "He said he bought sushi for breakfast!"

I laughed, but Mrs. Kawashiri took all talk about eating seriously. She rushed to a shelf and grabbed a plastic bag. It had a couple of pastries bought from the bakery a few doors down. "Here, you have these for breakfast."

"I can't take this, Mrs. Kawashiri. Mariko was just teasing."

"You take this anyway," she said, thrusting the bag into my hand. "You have to eat right. You bachelors don't take care of yourself. What you need is a good wife to take care of you," Mrs. Kawashiri added, not too subtly. She fancied herself a matchmaker.

"You're right," I answered. "But don't you think Mr. Kawashiri is going to object when I steal you away from him for myself?"

Mrs. Kawashiri laughed and slapped my arm. "Be careful with this one," she said to Mariko. "He's such a devil that if you do marry him, you're going to have to watch him every second."

"That I agree with. The question is, is it worth putting up with watching him every second?" Mariko asked.

"Don't kid yourself. He's such a cutie-pie that it will probably be worth all the trouble he'll give you."

Blushing furiously, I asked, "Can I use your phone?"

"Of course, Ken-san! I don't know why you even bother asking. Please use it."

I beat a hasty retreat to the relative safety of the telephone hanging on the wall. I got the number of the Golden Cherry Blossom Hotel from information and dialed it as Mrs. Kawashiri returned to the customers in the shop. I heard the phone ring like some distant bee at the other end of the line.

"Hello, Golden Cherry Blossom Hotel." The voice had the professional cheerfulness of a well-trained operator.

"Can you tell me if you have a guest named Susumu Matsuda staying at the hotel?"

"Just one minute, please."

After a slight pause, the operator came back on the line. "Yes, we do. Would you like me to ring the room?"

"Yes, please."

The phone rang several times with no answer. I hung up. "No one home," I told Mariko. "I'll have to try later this evening."

I worked at the office until early evening, setting up the clues that would be used for the upcoming mystery weekend. I dashed out to the Ginza Gardens Coffee Shop for a bowl of noodles for dinner and returned to the office to work some more.

Each of the clue givers in a mystery weekend has an instruction sheet written up for him or her. The sheet gives biographical information about their character, what their attitude is about the crime, and what key pieces of information they're supposed to give to the people trying to solve the mystery. Except for the "murderer," the clue givers normally don't know the total picture, so they can't give away too much inadvertently. Sometimes the player has to ask the right question, or to mention the right person or event to get the information. This means you have to juggle a lot of different elements when writing up the individual "rap sheets" for the clue givers.

Frankly, my mind wasn't really on the fictitious case I was creating. Instead, it kept drifting to the very real events of the day and the commission I received from Rita Newly. I turned her story over and over in my mind, and came to the conclusion that either Rita's story was genuine, or I was being set up to act as a courier in a drug buy or some similar illegal activity. Either possibility gave me a jolt of excitement tinged with fear. Against my better judgment, I welcomed both.

Going through with the package pickup for Rita Newly had the possibility of real danger. Some people might think that living in L.A. is dangerous enough, but for a lot of reasons I needed something more in my life, and this need clouded my judgment. Except for my relationship with Mariko, I was drifting. It was not a comfortable position to be in.

Like the generation before me, I had expected to reap the rewards of my education and experience in my forties. Instead, I was facing an uncertain future and the potential for increasingly difficult employment opportunities as I aged. It sometimes made me frustrated and angry. Frustrated and angry people sometimes do foolish things, like welcome a whiff of danger.

I told myself I'd be cautious, and seek out the police if it looked like I was involved in anything shady, but the truth is I found the aroma of real adventure an intoxicating perfume that dulled my senses. Maybe I should have taken up bungee jumping.

When I finished working on the clues I walked over to the Golden Cherry Blossom Hotel and entered the lobby a little after eight. It was close to the office so I didn't call ahead. The compact lobby was elegant and reminded me of a ship, with dark green carpet, dark wood panels, and fittings of polished brass.

"Can I help you, sir?" The Japanese behind the desk was impeccably dressed in a gray and green uniform. Wire-rimmed glasses perched on his nose, and perpetually upturned eyebrows gave his face a quizzical expression.

"Do you have a house phone? I'd like to call one of your guests."

"Certainly, sir. Right over there."

I walked to the house phone and picked it up.

"May I help you?" the operator's voice cut into the dial-tone.

"Would you ring Mr. Susumu Matsuda's room, please?"

"Certainly, sir."

The phone rang three times before it was picked up. "Yes?" The voice was remarkably free of accent. Since Rita said Matsuda came from Japan, I expected him to have more of a Japanese accent. Instead his English was flawless.

"Mr. Matsuda?"

"Yeah."

"My name is Ken Tanaka. I've been asked to pick up a package from you by Rita Newly."

"You say your name is Tanaka?"

"That's right. Ms. Newly asked me to pick up the package you have for her."

"When do you want to pick it up?"

"As a matter of fact, Mr. Matsuda, I'm in the lobby of the hotel. If it's not inconvenient, I'd like to come up right now and pick it up."

There was a long pause. I almost thought that I had been disconnected. Finally Matsuda said, "Okay. Come on up to room five-one-seven."

I hung up, looked around the lobby to get my bearings, and walked over to the elevator. After a few seconds one of the three elevators opened. I got in and punched the fifth floor button. On the fifth floor the hall had a gray and green carpet, green wall paper, and dark wooden doors. It was supposed to be elegant but I actually found it kind of dark and depressing.

I came to 517 and knocked. I could hear the murmur of voices behind the door—a man's and a woman's. I waited a minute and knocked a second time.

"Just a second." The man's voice.

They seemed to be arguing about something, but I couldn't make out what they were saying. Finally, after several minutes delay, the door was opened.

Standing before me was a Japanese man in his late sixties or early seventies. I was surprised at his age because I expected someone much younger. His gaunt face had the look of a wolf to it. He wore the stereotypical Japanese businessman's dark suit, white shirt, and dark tie. His hair was thinning and shot with gray. His expression was stern and suspicious. On his left cheek was a large, brown discoloration or birthmark.

"Mr. Matsuda?"

"Yes."

"I'm Ken Tanaka."

"Okay. I have the package," he said. "Come in for a moment."

I stepped into the room. Against the wall was a queen-sized bed with a dark green comforter on top. Two pictures of the "shopping-center-parking-lot-art-sale" school of art adorned the wall. A lamp, a television, a clock-radio, a small round table, and two chairs formed the rest of the furniture in the room. Standard hotel issue.

"Rita sent you?" Matsuda said suspiciously.

"Yes, she did."

"All right," Matsuda said. "I want some kind of receipt."

"That's no problem." I reached into my jacket pocket and pulled out one of the Kendo Agency business cards. On the back of the card I scrawled, "Received one package from Mr. Matsuda—K. Tanaka." I put the date on it.

While I was writing the receipt, Matsuda put a large wheeled suitcase on the bed. He unlocked the suitcase, opened it, and reached into it and pulled out a brown envelope. The envelope was sealed and tied with string—the pale, white, cellophane-like string that I've seen on packages from Japan.

I handed over the business card and accepted the package from Matsuda. He studied what I had written and seemed satisfied.

Just as I turned to leave, the door to the bathroom burst open. A short Latina came bustling out. Her hair was dyed a flaming orange and she wore a tight purple dress that clashed with the hair color.

"I'm tired of waiting in there," she announced as she strutted out of the bathroom. "I don't see why I have to be locked up in the john just so you can handle a little business."

She was wearing several rings on her hands, as many as three to a finger. She even wore a couple of rings on each of her thumbs. The scoop neck on her dress revealed two large breasts, and the tight fit across her hips picked up the curving theme of the bosom.

"Say, you're kind of cute, honey," the woman said, looking me over.

I was flustered by the unexpected outburst and looked at Matsuda for guidance.

Matsuda's face was tight with anger, not embarrassment. He said to the woman, "I thought I told you to wait in the bathroom until I was done with my business."

"Listen, honey, I got tired of waiting in there. I told you I didn't wanna go in there in the first place. We ain't got nothing to hide. Besides, I could give you guys a special deal on a little three-way party."

The woman gave me a toothy grin. I noticed the cracked lipstick around the edges of her mouth. She might have been in her mid-thirties, but it was hard to tell with all the makeup she had on. She could easily be older or younger. I was both surprised and amused by her sudden appearance. I hoped that I'd be as sexually active as Matsuda appeared to be when I reached my sixties or seventies.

"Well, how about it? Care to join a little fun? We can party until ten-thirty or so, then I got ta get dressed and leave 'cause I got to be on stage waving my G-string by eleven." She stopped and gave a short pirouette. She wore black patent leather shoes with tall spike heels. Her dancer's twirl was surprisingly graceful and polished.

"He's not here to join us," Matsuda said in a tight voice. "In fact, he's just leaving."

"That's too bad, honey" the woman said. "I think you'd have made quite an addition to our party."

I smiled from reflex and, clutching the envelope tightly to me, I slid past her toward the door. "It's nice of you to say so, but Mr. Matsuda's right. I really should be going. I believe we've accomplished our business. Thank you, Mr. Matsuda. I hope this contains everything that Ms. Newly expects it to contain."

"Sure it does," Matsuda said dryly. "If it doesn't, I'll be in Los Angeles for at least three more days and she can contact me."

"I'm sure she will if everything she's expecting is not here. Well, good night." I nodded to both Matsuda and the woman, and let myself out.

Outside of the room I had to control myself so I didn't start laughing. The look on Matsuda's face when the woman burst out of the bathroom was priceless. Even though Matsuda looked old,

I guess he was still frisky. Maybe it's all the green tea they drink in Japan. I had a good story to tell Mariko the next time I saw her.

My car was parked about five blocks away from the hotel. There was a cab line with two cabs in it in front of the hotel and I thought briefly of taking one to my car. During the day you're panhandled in downtown L.A., but at night some parts of the city are transformed into homeless tent cities that block the sidewalk. On darkened curbs drug deals also go down. Neither activity seemed like something I wanted to wander into, but I decided to walk. During the American Civil War an officer observed a man running from the front lines of battle and challenged him by asking why he was running. "Because I don't have wings to fly!" the man shouted as he ran past. That's exactly how I felt making my way through the darkened streets of downtown L.A. to my car.

When I reached my car I sat in it for a few moments examining the package under the weak dome light. The package was made out of glossy, thick brown paper. It was about seven by ten inches, but slightly odd in proportion, which I thought was because it was made to centimeter specifications, instead of inches like most envelopes I was familiar with. The envelope was about an inch thick and didn't feel very heavy.

I flexed the package. It felt like there were several sheets inside. I was puzzled.

I had a strange feeling in the back of my mind about the whole arrangement with Rita and Matsuda. Despite what I had told Mariko, it was simply too good to be true. Five hundred dollars seemed like too much money to pay for me to walk a few blocks and act like an errand boy. I was convinced that Rita Newly might be trying to get me involved with a drug pickup.

Because of this, I had resolved to open the package when I received it, just to make sure that I wasn't being used as a dupe for some illegal transaction. Now the size and weight of the package puzzled me. It could actually be the photographs and negatives that Rita had talked about.

I pursed my lips and thought about the ethics of the situation. When I thought I might be picking up a package of drugs, there was no hesitation in my mind that I would open the package. Now that there seemed to be a possibility that Newly's story might be true, I was hesitant.

Bouncing the envelope in my hand, I stared at the package.

I wasn't at the hotel for what happened next, but I later talked to Nachiko Izumi and I feel as though I know exactly what transpired. It started the next morning in the maid's staging area. Like so many days that turn out to be traumatic, the start was normal and routine.

As was the custom at the hotel, the maids were all lined up in a row with the flair of a military unit. There were nine or ten of them and they all stood at attention as the steely-eyed head of housecleaning for the hotel made her inspection. Next to each housekeeper's cart was an Asian woman dressed in a white uniform. Piled high on the carts were fresh smelling linens, newly laundered towels, glossy plum colored boxes of matches with the Golden Cherry Blossom imprint, and plastic wrapped water glasses with stickers that proclaimed that the glasses were "Sanitized for your safety."

Most of the women were Japanese, as was the head of housekeeping. As the head walked down the line of maids, she looked rather like a Marshal of Napoleon reviewing an artillery battalion. She abruptly stopped in front of one of the carts and noticed with distaste that the cart had not been stocked with the geometric precision that the more experienced maids are capable of. "Straighten up those glasses in a neat row, and make sure the various types of towels are not mixed together on the cart," she ordered in an imperious tone.

A thick accent to her English rubbed off some of the sharp edges of her words, but it was plain she was not pleased, and the hapless maid scurried to do as she had been instructed.

As the head of housekeeping finished walking down the line she turned and gave the maids she supervised one last look. Then she gave a curt nod and said, "Okay. Let's get to work."

One of the maids went directly to the fifth floor. She started her routine by checking a clipboard with a computerized list of the rooms to be cleaned, and moved to the first room, pushing her cart down the green-carpeted corridor. The row of drinking glasses in the cart made a cheerful tinkling sound as they banged together, forming a descant to the squeaking baseline provided by a bad bearing in one of the cart's wheels.

The maid was Nachiko Izumi, and the sound of the wheel annoyed her. Ms. Izumi was twenty-nine years old and in the U.S. less than five months. She was on a student visa and taking college classes in English literature and political science at East Los Angeles College. She was probably working without a green card, but working illegally is a kind of local sport in Los Angeles and I didn't ask her about this.

She approached number 517, and she didn't see the thin crescent of dark liquid peaking out from under the edge of the door. People had passed the room all morning without noticing the encroaching stain.

She moved the cart to the door and knocked softly. After a few seconds, she knocked more forcefully, calling out, "Excuse me! Maid!" After another pause she called out, *"Sumimasen"* (excuse me). Many of the clientele of the Golden Cherry Blossom are visiting Japanese tourists and businessmen, so she called out in both English and Japanese before entering the room. Finally, after going through the entire ritual required of her, she inserted her passkey into the door and unlocked it.

As the door opened, her attention was immediately drawn to the dark stain on the carpet and the object that lay just inside the open doorway. She stared at the object for several seconds, her brain not processing what her eyes were seeing.

Lying in a circle of blood was a severed human forearm and

what was left of a hand. Two fingers of the hand were missing, cleanly sliced off. The stub of the forearm, cut just below the elbow joint, was a pulpy mass of raw flesh, severed veins and splintered bone. It had been hacked off.

Ms. Izumi stared at the arm and gradually comprehended the horror that greeted her in room 517. She started to scream. It was a long, wailing scream, and she told me it was a long time before she was able to stop.

That morning I parked my Nissan in the lot at Second and Main, paid my $3.50 for the day, and started walking the block and a half to the office. In a part of town where parking can cost $3.00 every twenty minutes, this lot was a real find. I had the still-unopened package tucked under my arm, and although the day was sunny and not yet too hot, I was a little grumpy.

Mariko didn't show up the night before, which disappointed me. I figured she was late at her acting class at the East West Players theater. The aspiring students tended to sit around and share dreams of glory after the class. For Asian actors, those dreams were especially tough to realize.

Mariko told me once that she was resigned to the obvious: as an Asian, she would be forever cast in "Asian" roles. She said, "It's frustrating to realize that I'll never get to play Desdemona or Lady MacBeth unless I'm cast as a novelty. And let's face it, Ken, the number of Asian roles are few and far between. The number of good Asian roles are even fewer."

One reason a place like the East West Players thrived was that it allowed an outlet for the fermenting creativity of Asian actors, writers, and directors. Almost all the plays done by East West were written by Asians for Asians. Because of this, however, they have a limited audience and limited commercial value. Mariko's ambition to make a living at acting would never be realized at a small company like East West. In the commercial world, the world of mainstream television and movies, the number of paying jobs for Asians could typically be counted on the fingers of one hand during any given month.

"The odds of any actress making it are pretty slim," she once said to me, "so it's not like only Asians have a hard time." She was tough in her own way, and very determined. I think that toughness motivated her to fight her problem with alcohol and join AA. In AA you make a commitment to change your life. Stopping the drinking was only a part of that life change. I liked her courage. I was trying to decide what to do with the rest of my life, and in Mariko I could see a model for someone who was bootstrapping her life, changing it, and following her dream. I admired her. Maybe my problem was I had no dreams beyond finding another job.

As I approached the office I saw a white Mercedes sports car coming down Second Street. The top of the car was down, and behind the wheel, with her hair blowing in the wind, was Rita Newly. She looked like a scene out of a trite car commercial.

I was about to wave to her when I saw the expression on her face change to alarm. She was looking at two men who were standing in front of the office building. Both were Asians. One was a thin, slight man dressed in an expensive looking double-breasted suit. The other man was bulky to the point of being ape-like, with thick shoulders and a boxy head, shaved bald. His suit looked like it was tailored by Kmart. They straightened up when they saw Rita's sports car, and waved at her. The big man was missing half of his baby finger on the hand he waved with, and it looked peculiar when contrasted to the almost delicate, fully formed hand of the small man waving next to him.

Heedless of the oncoming traffic, Rita quickly spun the big wheel on the Mercedes and flipped a U-turn. Brakes squealed, horns sounded, and the drivers of other cars started cursing in a jarring mixture of English, Spanish, and Japanese, but Rita made her turn without a scratch.

The two men ran toward a blue Ford sedan parked in front of the building. They jumped in the car and also made a U-turn from their parking spot to pursue Rita, who was already half a block down Second Street. Cars, which had just started moving forward again after Rita's maneuver had stopped them, once again jammed on brakes and blared their horns.

I stood on the sidewalk watching the disappearing cars, washed by alternating waves of concern and puzzlement.

When I finally got to the office I tossed the package on the desk. I couldn't come up with a good reason for opening it. It obviously contained papers of some kind, but I figured whatever was in the package was Rita's business and not mine, even though I still didn't believe the story about photographs.

About an hour later the phone rang.

"Hello?"

"Mr. Tanaka?"

"Yes." I recognized Rita's voice. It sounded like she was on a car phone.

"Did you get the package?"

"Yes I did, but . . ." I was about to ask her what was going on with the two men and the cool maneuvers with the cars, but she quickly rushed forward.

"Look, I can't come in this morning to pick up the package. I want you to make sure that you put that package in a safe place. I might not be able to come in today at all."

"Sure, but I don't understand. Why do you want me to put some . . ." I was cut off by Rita's voice. This time her voice had an edge to it. She was very nervous.

"Please do as I say. In view of the fee I'm paying you, I think I should be able to ask for some special consideration when I make a request."

"Well, of course, Ms. Newly, but . . ."

"Thank you very much Mr. Tanaka. I'll be contacting you later when I can come by and pick up the package."

"But . . ."

"I can't talk anymore. Good-bye."

I sat listening to a dial tone. I picked up the package and looked around the office. I could bury it in a file cabinet or stick it in one of the desk drawers, but both were almost empty because they were essentially props. Maybe I should be clever and tape it to the back of one of the pictures hanging on the wall. Finally I decided the best thing I could do would be to get the package out of the office and leave it someplace nearby, where I could get to it easily.

I checked my watch. The boutique would open in a few minutes. I stuck the package under my arm and strolled out, locking the door behind me.

When I got to the boutique I could see Mariko and Mrs. Kawashiri inside arranging the stock hanging from chrome poles. I rapped on the door, pressed my nose flat against the glass, and put on a forlorn look. Mariko looked over to the door and jerked her thumb to indicate that I should take off. I shook my head and rapped once more on the glass.

Feigning exasperation, Mariko went to the door and opened it. "What now?" she said. "You're getting to be a pest."

"I came to beg a favor."

"What is it?"

I took the package out from under my arm. "Can you keep this here in the shop for me?"

"Sure," Mariko said. "But why?"

"Just call it a special request. I want to keep it nearby, but I don't want to keep it in the office."

"All right," Mariko said. "The big-time detective fan is getting mysterious."

"I missed you last night."

Mariko's face softened. "I'm sorry, Ken. We got caught up in acting class, and then afterward we were building sets for the new production. It was past one o'clock before I even knew it. I was dead tired, so I just went back to my place."

"Well, okay. But how about dinner tonight? My treat."

"Sure. This will be the first time you've taken me out to dinner in weeks, so you know darn well I'm not going to pass up a free meal. Besides, now that you've got me acting like Federal Express," she hefted the package in one hand, "I expect to be paid something for it."

"Federal Express delivers packages," I corrected her. "I just want you to hold this."

"Ken-san," Mrs. Kawashiri came up to us with a ready smile.

She had a warm heart for all strays and stragglers. To her, I suppose I fell under both categories. "It's so nice to see you. Come here," she said, holding up a white paper package. "Take one of these cinnamon buns for breakfast. I just got them from the bakery. They're freshly baked. They're good."

"I don't know, Mrs. Kawashiri. You're always giving me pastries and I feel guilty. In fact, you just gave me some yesterday. Besides, I shouldn't be here bothering Mariko."

"No. No. It's okay," Mrs. Kawashiri insisted. "Now, come here." She waved the sack in front of me. "You take this. You've been looking kind of thin lately. Now, come on. Take this."

Like a little boy, I marched up to the older woman and accepted the sack of pastries. "Thank you. This is real nice of you," I said.

"Anytime," Mrs. Kawashiri insisted.

"Lately it's been every time, Mrs. Kawashiri. The pastries are wonderful, but you can't keep giving me something every time I show up here."

She gave a snort that clearly indicated my protest was too silly to even discuss and turned around and went back to the racks of clothes.

"I've got to help Mrs. Kawashiri," Mariko said. "Is there anything else you want me to do besides hold this package."

"No," I said. I held up the bag of cinnamon buns. "Thank her again for me, would you?"

"Sure," Mariko said. "I may be a little jealous. She seems to like you more than I do. She's always feeding you, anyway."

"Pick you up at closing time," I called out over my shoulder.

Mariko smiled. "Sure. See you then."

When I returned to the office I saw a uniformed Los Angeles Police Department officer and a man in a suit standing in front of the door. The man in the suit looked like a football player, with sandy hair and a stern face marred by a nose broken in some distant altercation or scuffle. He looked like a cop, too, just not one who advertised it with a uniform. Both men watched me carefully as I approached the office.

"Can I help you with something?" I asked.

"Are you Mr. Tanaka?" the man in the suit asked.

"Yes, I am."

"Mr. Ken Tanaka?"

"That's right."

"Kendo Detective Agency?"

"Well, that's sort of a joke. It's not really a detective agency."

"A joke?"

"Sort of. It's part of an L.A. Mystery Club weekend puzzle."

"Puzzle? Mystery Club?"

"It's sort of a long story."

"My name's Detective Hansen, LAPD." He flashed an I.D. at me. "This is Patrolman Wilson. Maybe we can sit down for a few minutes and you can tell us this story."

"Sure. Why don't you come in?" I unlocked the door and motioned the two men in. Hansen went in but the patrolman waited until I preceded him before entering himself. I suppose it was to make sure I didn't run away. I went over to the desk and sat down. I motioned to the seat in front of the desk for Hansen.

"No, thanks," Hansen said.

Wilson, the one in uniform, stood by the door, blocking the exit. Hansen wandered around the office looking at the pictures on the wall and the furnishings in the office.

Despite my interest in mysteries, I've had minimal contact with police officers. I was fascinated to see that they acted very much like the police you see in movies and TV shows. I don't know if this was because art imitates life or life imitates art.

"You said you had a story to tell us," Hansen prompted.

I was puzzled, but not alarmed. I shrugged. "I belong to a club called the L.A. Mystery Club. Once a month we set up a fictitious mystery where club members act out parts in the mystery or try to solve the crime based on clues provided. It's sort of a cross between a game and a play."

"And this office?"

"The office is part of a mystery that I'm setting up for the next puzzle. I've only had it for a week."

"Are you a licensed detective, Mr. Tanaka?"

"No, I'm not. As I've been explaining to you, this whole setup is part of a club I'm with."

"Are you aware that to be a licensed detective in the state of California, a person is required to have two thousand hours of experience as a detective with a police force or a law firm?" Hansen finished circling the office, and sat down at the edge of the desk. I decided he was an officious ass.

"No, I didn't. Look, if I'm in any trouble because of the sign on the window . . ."

"Do you know a Mr. Matsuda, Mr. Tanaka?" Hansen didn't let me finish. I almost smiled at the familiar ploy. Except for the very real uniformed officer blocking the doorway, it could be part of an L.A. Mystery Club puzzle.

"I actually know several Matsudas. It's a common Japanese name."

"Mr. . . . . excuse me," Hansen reached into his pocket and pulled out a slip of paper, "Mr. Susumu Matsuda of Tokyo, Japan."

"I met Mr. Matsuda last night, but I can't say that I really know him."

Hansen pulled out two folded sheets of paper from his jacket pocket, and handed them over to me. I unfolded them and looked at the sheets. They were photocopies of my detective business card, both the front and the back.

"Is that your business card?" Hansen asked.

"It's one I had made up for the mystery puzzle. It goes along with the office."

"Is that your handwriting on the receipt on the back of the business card?"

"Yes, it is."

"Can you tell me what kind of package you received?"

"I don't honestly know. I picked up the package for a client and that was my only contact with Mr. Matsuda. I couldn't have spent three minutes in his room."

"A client?"

I sighed. I was beginning to feel very flustered. "A woman stopped by yesterday and apparently made the same mistake you did. She thought I was a real detective. She asked me to go to Matsuda's room and pick up a package for her."

"His room?"

"I visited him at the Golden Cherry Blossom Hotel. He's a guest there."

"When was this visit?"

"Last night."

"What time last night?"

"I don't know. I suppose a little bit after eight."

"And you only stayed there a few minutes."

"Yes."

"Was Mr. Matsuda alone?"

"As a matter of fact, he wasn't. There was a woman in the room with him."

"A woman?"

"That's right."

"Did you happen to learn her name?"

"No, I didn't."

"Was she there to pick something up, too?"

I shrugged. "I'd say she was there on quite different business, if you understand what I mean."

"No, I don't understand. What do you mean?"

"I believe she was a prostitute."

"What would make you suspect that she was a prostitute?"

"Some of the statements she made and the way she acted and looked."

"And you claim that this was the first time you met Mr. Matsuda?"

"That's right."

I knew what Hansen was doing. It was a cat and mouse game that I had played on more than one occasion myself in solving mystery weekend puzzles. Except in those circumstances I was usually the cat, and the person I was talking to was the mouse.

What made me the cat was knowledge—knowledge about the crime. When I did it, what I was trying to do in my questioning of the mouse was to draw some additional piece of knowledge or some statement that would connect the mouse to the crime.

It's amazing how strong the need to confess is in people. Sometimes, but not always, the cat and mouse game would lead the mouse to blurt out some confession. The confession might be only a half-truth, without the mouse actually saying he or she was guilty. But it was from those half-truths that a bridge could be built, piece by piece, between the crime and the person suspected of committing the crime.

I wondered what the crime was that Hansen was investigating, and although I thought it might be better to show patience until Hansen finally told me, I couldn't help myself and asked, "Can you tell me what this is about?"

"Earlier this morning Mr. Matsuda was found dead in his room."

There was a long silence. I was flabbergasted and for a confused moment I wished this was actually still part of some elaborate hoax arranged by some other member of the L.A. Mystery Club. Finally, Hansen said, "You don't seem very surprised."

"Actually, I'm stunned." Maybe I was hypersensitive, but I felt Hansen was doing the "inscrutable Asian" bit with his remark. It riled me. Now it was my chance to let the silence linger.

Hansen finally broke the silence by saying, "Did someone see you enter or leave Mr. Matsuda's room?"

"I asked the desk clerk about a house phone when I entered the hotel. The woman with Mr. Matsuda saw me leave. I don't know if any of the other hotel personnel saw me leave the hotel."

"How did you spend the evening after you saw Mr. Matsuda?"

"Went home, took a bath, read, and went to sleep."

"Any witnesses to that? You didn't see anybody or meet anybody later that evening?"

"No. I was alone."

"Where do you live, Mr. Tanaka?"

"Silver Lake, near Dodger stadium."

"Do you have a car?" In Los Angeles, this was almost a given. Hansen was making a statement more than asking a question.

"Yes, I do."

"Can you tell me where it is?"

"In the lot that's about a block and a half from here."

"Do you mind if we look it over?"

"For what?"

"We'd just like to look it over."

To see if they can find any clues, I thought.

"And my apartment?"

"Yes. That would be nice if we could get your address and permission to look it over."

I got scared. And with fear came anger. "You can look over anything you can get a warrant for."

"That's not being very cooperative."

"I don't have to be cooperative. It might not be in my best interest to be cooperative."

"Something to hide?"

"I believe you're the one who's been hiding things, or at least not telling me exactly what happened to Matsuda. So far you've told me he's dead. You've been interested in my whereabouts later last evening, even though I've admitted that I saw him. And you want to check out my car and maybe my apartment. What happened up there?"

"Mr. Matsuda was murdered. Very brutally murdered. In fact, he was more than murdered, he was totally dismembered; hacked to pieces. Our preliminary estimation is that it occurred at about one or two A.M., and it was such a brutal murder that whoever did it must have been covered with blood when he left the hotel. That's why I think it might be advisable to look over your car and possibly your apartment. In fact, since you're the first person we've come across who saw him last night, I think I'd like to ask you to come down to the station to make a statement."

8

Hansen sat in a small room directly opposite me. Between us was a metal table covered with linoleum. At one corner of the table there was the microphone of a tape recorder, positioned unobtrusively. On Hansen's side of the table was a large manila envelope. It had been a long afternoon.

"All right," Hansen said. "Let's go through your story one more time."

He had taken off his jacket and loosened his tie. The bright light from the fluorescent tubes in the ceiling framed his head and high-lighted the fact that he was starting to go bald. The closely cropped hair had a definite shiny spot at the back of his head. Hansen had combed his remaining hair forward and to one side to help cam-ouflage the receding hairline at the temples. His face was broad, with a wide chin. The scars of an adolescent problem with acne still pitted his cheeks.

I had already come to dislike Mr. Hansen intensely. He had a condescending manner that just made me bristle. I was raised to respect authority and to view good cops as heroes. Hansen may have been a good cop, but in my opinion he was a lousy human being. In life you come across all sorts of people. Some you like, some you don't like, and most you don't have strong feelings about one way or another. It's terrible when you come across someone you instantly don't like who has some power over your life. Hansen fit this description perfectly.

"You say you met Matsuda around eight?"

"That's right."

"And that he was not alone."

"No. He had a woman in the room with him."

"And that you took the woman to be a prostitute?"

"She acted like a prostitute. At least some of the things she said certainly suggested it. She said something about being a dancer, and even did a little pirouette."

"Like a ballet dancer?"

"Yes, but she didn't look like that kind of dancer. I told you she said something about waving a G-string, and the last time I looked ballet dancers don't wear G-strings." Hansen didn't like my sarcasm, and I told myself that I shouldn't let my dislike for him push me into acting like a smartass. "She had dyed red hair, was short, and a little plump. I've gone through this story twice before and told you exactly what she said."

"You didn't tell me about the little pirouette before. Just co-operate with us, Mr. Tanaka."

"I'm sorry." I shrugged. "I know you're going over and over my story to see if it's too pat, and therefore memorized, or too full of holes, and therefore inconsistent. But I've told you the truth and no matter how many times we go over the story it will come out more or less the same way each time."

Hansen tapped the table with his fingers in irritation. He absently reached to his shirt pocket where he had a pack of Marl-boro cigarettes. He caught himself and actually scowled. Early in the interview he had asked me if I minded if he smoked. In the cooped-up little room I most certainly did mind, and Hansen had now gone a couple of hours without a smoke. "Let's try a differ-ent topic for a while then. Why don't you tell me more about this club that you belong to?"

"The L.A. Mystery Club is a group of mystery enthusiasts who get together monthly to solve crimes."

"Crimes?" Hansen's eyebrows angled quizzically.

"Not real crimes," I added. "Some members of the club create the crime that's going to be solved. The other members come on a Saturday and follow a trail of clues to see if they can solve the crime. Afterward there's a dinner where the winners are announced and the solution is revealed."

"So it's sort of like kids playing Let's Pretend," Hansen said.

"No. It's adults solving intellectual puzzles. Sometimes quite complicated intellectual puzzles. But to solve these puzzles you pretend to be something that you're not. To solve the puzzles some members play roles like in a play. Sometimes we even hire professional actors. They act the parts of various characters in the mystery. The other members sometimes act out the parts of various favorite detectives."

"Like what?"

"Like Sherlock Holmes or Miss Marple, characters from detective literature. People like that."

"It all sounds kind of silly to me," Hansen said.

"Most recreation is. With you, solving crimes is a profession. With us, it's a hobby. There's a difference in your outlook when you're doing something just for the fun of it."

"It seems like there's a more important difference," Hansen said. "All these club crimes are just foolishness. What I've got on my hands is a real murder."

I felt my face burn red. I hated Hansen's attitude, and his remarks about the childishness of the L.A. Mystery Club were all the more infuriating because they had a germ of truth to them. Despite this truth, I felt my anger toward Hansen growing. In the back of my mind I wondered if this was a technique Hansen was using in an effort to make me lose my temper and perhaps say something that I normally wouldn't.

"So because of this club activity, you rented the office and had business cards made up," Hansen continued.

"Yes." My voice now had a brittleness caused by anger.

"And you claim that this woman, Rita Newly, showed up at your office by mistake."

"I assume it was a mistake. Initially I thought it might be another member of the L.A. Mystery Club playing a trick on me."

"But it wasn't."

"Obviously not."

"So she hired you to go get the package from Matsuda?"

"That's right."

"And you decided to play detective and do it."

Once again I felt my face turning red with embarrassment and anger. My jaw clenched and I spat out, "Yes."

"So apparently you weren't able to differentiate between your little playacting and reality?"

"Apparently."

"You didn't get Newly's address or telephone number?"

"No."

Hansen sighed and sat back in his chair. "Not much of a detective, are you?"

"Apparently not."

"By the way, what did you do with the package?" Hansen asked.

"I gave it to her," I lied.

"Rita Newly?"

"The woman who called herself Rita Newly." My anger made me lie about the disposition of the package, and I knew it was a mistake to make such a foolish statement as soon as the words were out of my mouth. I was about to retract the lie when I saw Hansen shaking his head with a patronizing smirk.

"So essentially you were a delivery boy and not a detective."

"Yes, and please don't call me a boy. I'm a full-grown man." I stared at the black tube of the microphone sitting on the desk and wanted desperately to retract my lie, but I realized the entire interview was being recorded, and I didn't know how to extricate myself gracefully from the situation I had just put myself in without giving Hansen a chance for more snotty comments.

Hansen lifted up the manila envelope. "I want to show you something." He opened up the envelope and took out several large photographs. "These are pictures of the body and the room. Could you identify Matsuda if I showed them to you?"

"I only met him once. Aren't you sure he was the one who was killed?"

"The fingerprints and photo matched his passport, so we're sure who the victim was," Hansen said. "But I want you to look at the pictures to make sure the man in the room you met was actually Matsuda."

Hansen hesitated a second, then added, "It may be difficult to identify Matsuda's face. The body was pretty well cut up. The doctors say a lot of it was done after he was already dead. It was a pretty violent murder."

Hansen handed the photos to me. I looked at the first photo. My stomach gave an immediate lurch at the sight. It was in color; an eight-by-ten blowup.

Lying on the floor in a corner of the room, dressed in the same suit that I had seen him in, was the body of Matsuda, or what was left of it. Long red slices crisscrossed the head and shoulders, and flaps of skin, matted with blood and hair, hung loosely, exposing the white skull beneath. It was hard to identify the face with the multitude of slashes, but I could see a part of the birthmark on a patch of skin that still clung to the skull. Blood was splashed everywhere.

In my short time in Vietnam I can't say that I know for sure that I ever killed someone. I shot at people but I never actually saw anyone get hit. I did see several people killed, however, including someone blown to pieces by a land mine. It was his second day in Vietnam, and he was just unlucky. The horror of that ripped-apart body in Vietnam was no worse than the slashed body before me in the pictures. But for some reason the situation with Matsuda struck me as somehow more terrible. The body in Vietnam was mutilated by the effects of mindless energy during a time of war; an explosion set off because a foot was placed on the wrong patch of earth. The body in the picture was ripped to pieces because someone had stood before it and slashed at it over and over again.

In the picture, one of Matsuda's arms was twisted to one side, and the other arm was just a stump. A ring of blood soaked the end of the cut-off jacket sleeve where the rest of Matsuda's arm should have been.

I shuffled the pictures. The second picture explained the mystery of the missing arm. Lying on the green rug of the hotel room was the severed arm, with the hand mutilated and missing some fingers. It seemed to be resting just inside the doorway, where someone entering the room would see it first. Next to the arm was a little slip of paper with a number written on it. It was some kind of identification number used by the photographer.

I turned to another picture to see one of the severed fingers lying on the carpet in a closeup shot. The curly nap of the green carpet was clearly visible, with the brown severed finger lying incongruously on it like some red and tan slug crawling across a curly green sea bottom. Another identification number flanked the finger.

The last picture was a closeup of the face. The flesh was sliced by dozens of blows that exposed bloody muscle and bone. I glanced at it without focusing on what I was seeing. I handed the pictures back to Hansen.

"It's unbelievable," I said, shaken.

"It's not unbelievable because it happened. That's the difference between your recreation and my job. The blows on the hands and wrists are characteristic of defense wounds; someone placing their hands and arms over their head to protect themselves. That's how the fingers got sliced off and how the arm was hacked off, too. You can see the defense mechanism didn't do much good, because even after Matsuda was dead someone continued to hack away at his head. The forensics boys say it was probably done with a long, sharp instrument. Maybe a sword."

"A sword? It must be a maniac."

Hansen shrugged. "Who knows. Some people do worse things for just a few bucks. But this was pretty bad. Whoever did this was not someone with just a casual grudge against Matsuda."

"I can't identify the face with all the head wounds, but it's the same suit that Matsuda was wearing when I saw him earlier that evening, and I saw part of a birthmark on Matsuda's cheek. Or at least that part of the cheek that is still attached to the skull."

"And after seeing these," Hansen said, touching the photographs, "do you have anything else you want to say to us about what happened?"

I shook my head, too upset to even remember my lie.

When I finally got out of Parker Center, the main police head-quarters in L.A., I wanted to pick up Mariko, tell her what had happened, and ask her for advice.

9

I don't think Americans are an especially honest people. Cheating on taxes is endemic, and everyone speeds over sixty-five miles per hour. I admit to the latter, but I'm too scared to do the former. I used to have a friend call me every April to boast how little he was paying in taxes. He accomplished this through outrageous cheating, and he was proud of it. He stopped calling the year I told him that because of cheating bastards like him, stupid bastards like me were paying more taxes.

We like to think we're honest, and old Frank Capra movies celebrate the innate honesty of Americans. We're decent and frank and open and we often confuse all these traits with real honesty. Maybe Americans were more honest when Capra made movies in the 1930s, but now honesty is not as celebrated as shrewdness. Top government officials circumvent the law when it suits them, and Savings and Loan executives, lawyers, and car salesmen have the reputation for being so crooked that these professions have become a shorthand for what Capra would have called "sharp dealing." It's sad, but there you have it.

Having said all this, I must admit I was shredded by remorse about not telling Hansen the truth about the package. Dickens once said, "The law is an ass." I thought Hansen was a supercilious ass, but he was still the law.

Mariko curled into the curve of my arm. We were both sitting on my dilapidated couch with our feet up on my equally dilapidated coffee table. "I've got to tell him about the package tomorrow," I said.

Mariko looked thoughtful. "I think you've got to talk to my cousin Michael, first."

"The lawyer?"

"Yes. Get his advice first, then tell Hansen about the package."

"You really think that's necessary? Consulting a lawyer, I mean?"

"You're the one who was hauled downtown to talk about the murder. You let them look over your car and you sat for hours talking to them. You probably should have had a lawyer then and you shouldn't have given up your rights, because you told me you certainly knew them. You said that Hansen rubbed you the wrong way. He's just looking for a suspect in the murder and you might be it, Ken. I think you better get Michael's advice before you just march down to the police and say you actually have the package."

"Correction: You've got the package."

"Well, it's at the boutique."

"Is it in a safe place?"

"Yeah, I've got it in a hatbox in the stockroom. It's safe, unless we get hit by a hat burglar, as opposed to a cat burglar."

"Very funny." I paused. "I'm sorry I got you involved in this," I told Mariko.

"Well, I am involved in it, at least because I have an investment in you that I don't want to see wasted. After all the work I've been putting into you, I don't want some gorilla named Bubba to reap the rewards of what I've done just because he ends up as your cell mate."

"Meaning?"

Mariko reached up and patted my cheek. "Meaning those nights in prison can get awfully long and lonely, and you might start looking awfully good to some of those guys in there."

"That's a comforting thought."

She smiled, "Well, it's something to think about. I might not be the only one that finds your sweet buns attractive."

I rolled my eyes.

"By the way, that Hansen guy sounds like a creep," Mariko continued.

"I guess he's just doing his job."

"Do you think he was so snotty because you're Japanese?"

That was an angle I hadn't resolved. Racism doesn't spring to mind whenever I have an unpleasant encounter with someone, but the insidious problem with racism is that once you've been stung by it you always have it lingering as a possibility.

When my marriage fell apart, I had a job programming at the Calcommon Corporation. With my personal life in shambles, I decided to concentrate on my career. I think now that I was embarrassed and hurt by the divorce more than I realized and simply wanted to divert my energies into something I viewed as an activity of the intellect instead of an activity of the heart.

Over time I noticed that I was not advancing in my career. Although my performance reviews were excellent, I was not made a supervisor or manager. I started taking business courses at UCLA in an effort to get into management, but that didn't seem to advance my career, either.

I used to think that the world is color-blind. Maybe that's my Hawaiian upbringing. Lately I've come to the frightening conclusion that race is becoming the defining factor of our lives. Maybe this is because I live in Los Angeles, which has degenerated into a collection of ethnic tribes instead of a community. Here all the racial groups are in deadly competition. Literally. This has consequences for all of us, no matter what our race is.

One consequence for me was the nagging doubt that maybe I wasn't being promoted at Calcommon because I was an Asian. It would have been a relief if some third party I trusted would just tell me I wasn't good enough to be made a manager, but that wasn't the case. The difficult assignments I got showed I was performing my job, and I had no problems working in teams. My performance reviews were always outstanding.

One day, out of curiosity, I took out a Calcommon organization chart and marked down the races and gender of the corporation's top management. There was one Latino (who was in charge of buying office supplies), one black (given the title of manager, but just in charge of the mail room), and only one woman (also given the title manager, but really in charge of employee activities like the annual picnic). The rest of Calcommon's management structure was lily white and male.

If you're a white male, this kind of research may bring a wince to your face. Some white males have been treated very unfairly in ham-fisted efforts to correct past racial and gender wrongs by perpetrating new wrongs. But traditional barriers to nonwhite and nonmale employees far exceed the new barriers to white males. That doesn't make any barrier right, but it does mean that if you're not a white male, you're probably more likely to come into contact with prejudice.

In my own country I've been called a gook, a chink, a Jap, and a slope. I think "gook" was first applied to Koreans, "chink" to Chinese, "slopes" to Vietnamese, and "Jap" is both obnoxious and obvious. Asians in the U.S. get to learn the full range of ethnic slurs, no matter what their real ethnicity is. I've also been told to go back to my own country, even though America has been home to my family since 1896.

Like many people, I'm tired of some people excusing their personal conduct because of past injustices to their race, religion, sexual preference, or gender. Despite that, racial prejudice was a possibility when faced with the situation I was in.

I talked to my immediate supervisor about promotion and Calcommon's racial policies, and he was very uncomfortable. He said he would talk to our department manager about my concerns, and eventually I was granted an interview with Calcommon's white, male vice-president of human resources. Mr. VP gave me the usual song and dance and said that if my performance warranted it, I would certainly be considered for a supervisory or management position.

And then a strange thing happened. A few months later I got my first mediocre performance review at Calcommon.

I was angry and upset, and I remember my immediate supervisor wouldn't look me in the eye when he gave me the review. I was transferred from software development to software maintenance. In the world of software, development is where the fun and challenge is. Maintenance is usually where you stick beginners and less-qualified programmers, who spend their days making minor changes to the work of others.

As I considered my options, the nagging voice of my mother reached out from the grave. Like a good second generation Japanese mother, she valued security above all else. When she was alive she'd counsel, "Don't make waves" or "Play along" or "Don't cause trouble," and to my undying shame, as soon as the anger passed, that's what I did.

About a year later Calcommon went through what the MBA types euphemistically call "downsizing," and I was cut. So much for playing safe and not making waves. Calcommon did give me a generous severance package, but I regarded that as a payoff for being a "model minority."

I was tired of being a model minority, but I didn't relish the thought of having to confess to Hansen that I had misled him about the package. I decided to take Mariko's advice and talk to her lawyer cousin Michael before I did anything more.

"You said the pictures of the body were pretty awful," Mariko said.

"They were. I bet the television crews were mad as hell they couldn't get into the room to film it."

"You're getting cynical in your old age."

"Age has nothing to do with it. I was always cynical. As I get older I'm just getting braver about showing it. You know blood and gore make for big ratings. The only thing missing is sex, and maybe the prostitute in Matsuda's room or Rita Newly will supply that." I paused. "It really was awful to see those pictures, Mariko. But the way Matsuda died is in itself a clue."

"What do you mean?"

"Well, the cops said that he was hacked up with something like a sword. People don't go running around with swords these days. It's hard to understand why you'd chose that weapon. Plus somebody had a real grudge against Matsuda or else they wouldn't have taken the time and effort to slice him up the way they did."

"It must have been a mess," Mariko said.

"It was. They didn't show me all the pictures, but I'm sure the entire room must have been splattered in blood. Whoever did it must have been covered in it. In fact, it's amazing that they were able to get out of the hotel without someone seeing them covered with blood."

Mariko touched my cheek. "You're shaking." We kissed. Her lips were cool and moist. I sank into their softness and, after a time, I stopped shaking. I'll spare you the active details of our sex life. Just think of pounding surf, rearing stallions, heavy rain, and any other sexual cliché you like from old movies.

When we were done with our lovemaking, during that period when women like to cuddle and men just want to drift into unconsciousness, Mariko said, "Did you forget about tomorrow night?"

That snapped me awake. Women and men sometimes have trouble communicating, but even the dullest man learns when a woman is broadcasting a signal. This was not a question; it was a test. Men hate these tests, but women keep giving them because we men seem to keep failing them. "Of course not. It's your first time speaking at an AA meeting, and I will be there for you," I said with aplomb.

She snuggled closer to me. The test was not only passed, it was aced.

10

The phone rang. I picked it up and recognized Mariko's voice. It was unusual for her to call me early in the morning.

"There's a big write-up about your murder in the *L.A. Times*," she said.

"My murder? If it's about my murder, then like Mark Twain said, my death has been greatly exaggerated!"

"Gee, the wonders of a sixth-grade education."

"Never mind the sarcasm. What are you talking about?"

"There's a big write-up in the *Times* about Matsuda's murder," Mariko said. "It talks about Matsuda and then discusses how other Japanese businessmen have been victimized by crime in Little Tokyo. You know, muggings and things like that."

"Why don't you read it to me?"

"Read it to you? It's about half a page long. It wouldn't kill you to go out and get a paper."

"Ever helpful."

"Well, I'm trying to be," Mariko answered. "I thought you might be interested in it. Besides, you're mentioned in the article."

"I am?"

"Sure, I'll read you that part, at least. 'The police say they are following up on various clues and checking out the stories of suspects.' I figure that's you," Mariko announced.

"You're not going to think it's so funny if it turns out to be true, and you end up bringing me gift baskets at some maximum security prison. Remember 'Bubba'?"

Mariko's voice was much less animated. "Do you think that will actually happen?"

"Well, I hope not. But it has happened in the past, and I certainly don't want to put it to the test in this case. You know the cops can start feeling the heat just like anybody else. And if there's a lot of pressure being put on Hansen to make an arrest, there's no telling what he might do."

"I was kidding."

"I hope you're kidding, too. I just want you to know you shouldn't go around joking about me being a suspect because it's probably true."

"Now you've got me worried sick," Mariko said.

"About me?"

"Of course."

"I thought you were worried that I might say that you were the mastermind behind the whole thing."

"Don't tease about this, Ken."

"I'm like you. I sort of vacillate between macabre humor and outright hysteria. I'll go down and read what the *Times* has to say about the case, then I'll call you back later this afternoon. Will you call your lawyer cousin and set up a time for me to see him? I want to get rid of the package as soon as possible."

"Okay."

"Oh, Mariko?"

"Yes."

"I love you."

"Finally some sense comes out of your mouth." She hung up.

I went down to the corner doughnut shop and got a *Times*. Back in my apartment I read the story about the murder. It had a short interview with Nachiko Izumi, the maid who found the body, but the actual details of the murder were pretty sketchy. I did learn that the police confirmed the weapon was probably a sword, based on the wounds inflicted on the body. And I was fascinated to read a little bit about Matsuda's background.

Matsuda had been raised in the United States, but he went to Japan right after World War II and renounced his U.S. citizenship. Since that time, he had been in the United States frequently, acting as a sales agent for a variety of companies.

The article went on to talk about other crimes in Little Tokyo, with visiting Japanese businessmen as their victims. The crime rate in the United States is much higher than in Japan, and despite a lot of publicity in Japan about it, many of the visitors simply weren't trained to cope with the Los Angeles urban jungle.

A favorite technique seemed to be going from room to room in hotels that catered to the Japanese businesspeople, knocking on doors and mugging or robbing the residents when they opened the door to see who was there. Welcome to America.

After reading the paper and having some breakfast (this time, cornflakes, not sushi), I decided to call Ezekiel Stein, the president of the L.A. Mystery Club. Ezekiel was a manager in the Water Quality Division of the L.A. Department of Water and Power (DWP). He was a thin man in his fifties, with a small beard and thick, black-rimmed glasses.

Ezekiel actually got me involved in the L.A. Mystery Club, and I met him in kind of a funny way. The Los Angeles DWP has this mania for covering open reservoirs. They like to take restful blue water and spread a plastic cover over it in the name of water improvement. In fact, the way to improve water is to filter it, not just cover it, but covering is cheap and the City of L.A. likes cheap.

Residents and environmentalists opposed the covering of the reservoirs, arguing that if the DWP really wanted to improve water quality they should take steps that will achieve that aim, instead of taking a halfway measure that destroyed the open reservoirs without making any substantive improvement in water quality. The Silver Lake district of L.A. got its name from the open reservoirs that form its geographic and emotional center. Like most people in Silver Lake, I joined the effort to stop the covering.

I met Ezekiel at a community meeting to discuss ways to keep the reservoirs uncovered. I noticed that Ezekiel had placed some flyers on a table when he entered the meeting, and I strolled over to see what they were. They advertised an upcoming L.A. Mystery

Club weekend event, and I talked briefly with Ezekiel about the event and what was involved. I was surprised when later I saw Ezekiel sitting as part of a panel representing the DWP. When you view people as part of the opposition on an issue, you don't often view them as having aspects to their lives that you might share an interest in.

I decided to give the mystery weekends a try and found them fun. As I got more involved with the club, I got to know Ezekiel better. I still thought his views about covering the reservoirs were a sacrilege, but I also learned that it shouldn't prevent me from working with him on things of interest to both of us.

Ezekiel was an engineer, which explained some, but not all, of his eccentricities.

For instance, for fun he would calculate the center of gravity for all sorts of things, such as automobiles or oranges. As near as I could tell, knowing the center of gravity is only useful for things like airplanes or sailboats, but Ezekiel calculated it for just about anything that struck his fancy: chairs, tables, phone booths, and myriad other objects. He once proudly showed me a database he kept on a laptop computer that had all his center of gravity computations, along with a scanned photo or sketch of the object. He had literally thousands of entries, and he told me he had been doing this since college.

Ezekiel would also get involved in long tiffs with bureaucracies (and L.A. has many, what with all the city, county, and state agencies, not to mention agencies with adjacent cities). If some bureaucratic rule seemed illogical to him, he would sometimes spend months trying to get it changed, even when the change he wanted seemed to have no practical effect. Working for the world's largest municipally owned utility, he should have known the difficulties in getting any bureaucracy to change, but he always had a half dozen little skirmishes going on.

His trait of most interest to me was his voracious reading about crime.

His phone rang and I heard the familiar voice answer, "Hello."

"Ezekiel. Ken Tanaka here. What do you know about recruiting American women to entertain in Japan?" With Ezekiel it was unnecessary to go through the normal social amenities. In fact, it was often counterproductive to do something like ask him how he felt. Ezekiel would tell you, in excruciating detail, including (I once learned to my sorrow) a report on his latest schedule of bowel movements and stool condition.

"There's been sporadic complaints about it. Often the Japanese don't comply with the terms of the contracts they sign with the women, which causes problems."

"Have you ever heard of a woman being blackmailed once she returned to the States?"

"Blackmail?" A pause. I could just see the gears turning in his mind while he thought about that one. "No, I've never heard of a case of blackmail once the woman returned to the United States. Why do you ask."

"I think I might be involved with one."

"You mean a real one?"

"Yes. And that's not the half of it. I'm also involved with that Japanese businessman that was killed at the Golden Cherry Blossom last night."

"The one reported in the *Times?*"

"Yes." I gave Ezekiel a brief rundown on my meeting with Rita and Matsuda. I left out the part about still having the package. When I was done, I asked, "Any ideas?"

"Obviously the woman didn't want to pick up the package herself because she was trying to put something over on Matsuda. For five hundred bucks she bought herself a sacrificial goat."

"So who killed Matsuda?"

"Not enough information," Ezekiel said. "Can't figure things like this out without information."

"Yeah, I'm finding that out," I said. "Say, do you know a good criminal lawyer?"

"I know of several lawyers who are criminals."

I gritted my teeth and rephrased my question. Ezekiel was not trying to be funny. When people laughed at things he said, he'd sometimes get puzzled and hurt. It was just the way his brain worked. "Do you know of any lawyers who are good at representing criminals?"

"Just what I read in the paper. Do you need one?"

"I might. Mariko has suggested her cousin Michael, but I don't know him and I want to make sure I talk to someone who knows what he's doing."

"You need Mary Maloney. That woman can find out anything. She'll know how to find out what you want to know about Mariko's cousin. Anything else?"

"No, not now."

"Okay, but talk to me more about this when you have the time."

The phone was dead. It was typical of Ezekiel to hang up without saying good-bye, and I wasn't offended by it. I replaced the receiver and decided to drive down to the detective office before I called Mary.

I parked my car in the lot I normally used and walked to the office. I noticed the posters advertising Little Tokyo's Nisei Week festival on the telephone poles. A *Nisei* is a second generation Japanese in the U.S. I was a third generation, which made me a *Sansei*.

Little Tokyo's Nisei Week celebration was started in 1934 by a bunch of enterprising Nisei looking for a way to drum up jobs. It usually coincided with the Japanese *O-bon*, which is held in late summer. Before coming to L.A., I had never heard of Nisei Week, but O-bon was something we used to celebrate in Hawaii. In the way we Americans have of homogenizing ethnic events until they lose their toothiness, the L.A. version of O-bon consists of a parade with street dancing, plus the usual kitsch things like a beauty pageant and plenty of chicken lunches for businessmen. I don't think most people know that the festival has its roots in a Buddhist religious festival.

I walked into the office building and summoned the slow elevator. The building where I rented the office had one supreme virtue: the rents were dirt cheap. Otherwise, it was a pit. Like most old office buildings, it had a smell of age clinging to it, like the stale ghost of the past. When the building was new and bustling with commerce it was home to dentists and lawyers and several small accounting firms. Now it housed small-time import/export businesses and nondescript enterprises with names like "John Smith, Inc."

My office was on the second floor, and in the few days I had occupied the office I rarely saw anyone else walking the halls of this floor. I put the key in the door and turned the lock.

The scene that greeted me was chaos. Every file cabinet drawer had been opened, removed from the cabinet, and dumped on the floor. The desk drawers had been treated in a similar fashion. Even the four pictures I had hung on the wall had been taken down and dumped facedown on the desk. It took me a few moments to realize that someone was looking at the backs of the pictures, to make sure nothing had been taped to them. So much for my idea to do precisely that with the package.

Since they were all props and stage furniture, most of the drawers were empty. The one exception was the top drawer of the desk, where I kept my notes about the mystery weekend, along with short biographies I had written for each of the characters in the mystery. These were scattered on the top of the desk. Someone had apparently read them and I wondered what they made of them.

The phone started ringing and I was at a loss to find it for a few seconds. I finally went to where the cord was plugged into the wall and followed the cord until I found the phone sitting under a file drawer. I sat on the floor and answered it.

"Hello?"

"Mr. Tanaka?"

"Yes."

"This is Rita Newly. I've been calling for two days now to make arrangements to pick up my property." Her tone was brittle and sharp.

"I'm sorry I haven't been in the office. A good part of the time I was with the police."

"The police?" Her tone was now more wary than surprised.

"Yes. Mr. Matsuda was murdered soon after I picked up the package for you."

"That has nothing to do with me," she said hastily. "The package is my property, and part of a normal business transaction."

"Pornography and blackmail are normal business transactions? That's a peculiar view of what you've told me."

"Look, I really need that package. What will it take to get you to give it to me?"

"How about starting with some information? For instance, who were those two Asians you were running away from yesterday morning?"

"What Asians?"

"Oh, come on, Ms. Newly. I was in front of the office when you pulled your cool maneuver with the Mercedes. It seemed precipitated by your seeing two Asian gentlemen standing in front of the office."

"I don't know who they were."

I sighed, exasperated. "If you didn't know them, why did you take off? They certainly seemed to know you because they took off after you. Now I come into the office and find everything turned upside down. . . ."

"What do you mean?"

"I mean someone ransacked my office yesterday afternoon or last night. Everything is torn apart."

"Did they get the package?"

"The famous package! No, they didn't get the package. It's being held at a safe place not five minutes from the office. But you're not going to get it until you start telling me the truth about what this is all about."

There was a long silence. "Hello?" I finally said, thinking she might have hung up.

"I'm sorry, Mr. Tanaka," she was all sweetness and light again. "Those men were Yakuza, Japanese gangsters. I recognized one from Tokyo. They scared me when I saw them in front of your office, and I just panicked and ran."

"Gangsters?"

"That's right."

I digested that statement. Lacking anything more insightful, I asked, "So, what's going on?"

"I don't know. My package has nothing to do with the murder of Mr. Matsuda. That shocked me when I heard about it on the news. But I'm sure my business with him has no connection with this crime."

So she already knew about Matsuda's murder. I wondered if she knew from the news or some other means. "So, what is your involvement in this?"

Another pause. "I'm not sure I can trust you," she said. "Can you let me think about it for a while and get back to you?"

"Why don't you give me a number where I can get in touch with you," I suggested.

"No, I'll call you," she said. She hung up.

"Damn!" I said as I slammed down the phone. I sat for a few minutes, but finally decided that the most positive way I could vent my frustration was to put the office back into order.

As I worked I came across the telephone books that I got when I installed the phone. I put them aside and finished putting the office together. When I was done I picked up the yellow pages and started flipping through them. Finding the woman in Matsuda's room was important. She could confirm my story about just being in the room a few minutes and leaving. She could also supply the cops with information on what happened after I left. The question was, how to find her?

Of course, Sherlock Holmes would have known her family history, her place of employment, her residence, and her social security number after a ten-second meeting, but unfortunately I wasn't The Great Detective. In fact, I wasn't even a great detective. Thinking about it, I wasn't even a detective. Great.

But I did have clues. She said she was a dancer, and she said she needed only half an hour to get dressed and on stage after her proposed "party." That meant she had to get someplace close to the hotel. Even at 10:30 at night, you can't drive too far in downtown L.A. in that time. She also said something about a G-string. In an age where some grandmas wear thong bikini panties, sexy underwear is not a big deal, but I imagine something like a G-string is still primarily worn by strippers. That meant a club or something similar. So I should have been able to narrow things down to a strip joint within a short driving distance from the hotel. So far, so good.

But how to pinpoint what strip joints were within a short distance of the hotel became a problem. I looked up strippers in the yellow pages and only found stripping telegram services. I looked up strip clubs and found nothing. Nightclubs got me a lot of listings, but no real indication about which ones had strippers. It looked as if I might be condemned to driving around the hotel in ever-widening circles, keeping my eyes peeled for someplace where the woman might be dancing. That seemed like a long and tedious task, but one that couldn't be avoided without some kind of listing of strip joints in downtown L.A.

The phone rang. It was Mariko.

"How's it going?" she asked.

"Uh, fine, I guess."

"Something's wrong."

"Somebody ransacked the office here."

"A thief?"

"Maybe, but they didn't seem to take anything."

"The package. They were looking for the package."

"Maybe. I can't be sure. It might be coincidence."

"Are you going to report it to the police?"

"I'm not sure about that, either. They didn't take anything, and I really hate that cop assigned to this case. He's an ass. Have you called your cousin Michael yet?"

"He's in court this morning. His secretary said he'd call back this afternoon. I said it was important."

I sighed.

"So what are you going to do?" Mariko asked.

"I'm trying to find the woman who was in Matsuda's room. She can verify my story."

"How are you going to do that?"

"Ah, research," I said lamely. I was embarrassed to tell Mariko of my fruitless investigation into strip joints.

"What kind of research? Are you going to cruise for hookers?"

That was a development I hadn't contemplated. In downtown L.A. that could be a formidable task. "If you must know, I was trying to figure out how to find the addresses of all the strip joints in downtown L.A. I want to plot them on a map and see which ones are close to the hotel. I haven't had much success, though, because strip joints aren't listed in the yellow pages."

"Oh, if that's what you want you should pick up a copy of the *L.A. Sizzle* newspaper. They sell them in front of liquor stores. It will have a complete listing of strip joints and bars with strippers."

"How do you know that?"

"I have my sources."

"Seriously, how would you know that?"

"Hey, the guys in AA have sworn off liquor, not vice. Most of those nude places can't serve hard liquor, so the guys claim it's a good place to hang out. Of course, something like the public library doesn't serve liquor, so I don't think not serving liquor is the real reason the guys go to the clubs."

I stammered my thanks to Mariko for the tip, then went a block to a liquor store that, sure enough, had a news rack with the *L.A. Sizzle* newspaper in front of it. On the way back to the office I looped past my car and got my Thomas Brothers map guide.

The newspaper had the ads for nude bars neatly organized by the section of the city, and it only took me a few minutes to locate two clubs close to the hotel, along with a theater called the Paradise Vineyard that promised "Old Time Burlesque" in its ad. I marked their locations on my map of downtown.

Since they were all close, I decided to drive by them to see what there was to see, but first, on impulse, I picked up the phone and called Mary Maloney.

When she found out who it was, Mary's voice warmed up. "Ken! How's the mystery coming? We're all looking forward to participating in it."

"It's coming along fine, but I have something more serious to ask you."

"Oh, what is it?" Mary was a large woman, who enjoyed mothering people. Maybe that's why she has contacts everywhere who were willing to help her whenever she wanted. Mary was still something of a puzzle to me. For all her openness and friendly demeanor, she really didn't talk much about herself. She didn't seem to work, and although she seemed to have a modest lifestyle, she also had a penchant for taking off to Europe or Asia for weeks at a time, seemingly on a whim. That implied some source of income, but she never talked about it. She also had a mania for knitted dresses, sweaters, and pants suits. In fact, I couldn't recall seeing her in anything that wasn't knitted. I don't know if she made these clothes herself or bought them, but Mariko once remarked that Mary's clothes were custom-made, and not off the rack.

"I'm afraid I'm involved with that murder at the Golden Cherry Blossom Hotel, and I need to get some legal advice about how to gracefully get out of a situation I've put myself in. Mariko has suggested that I talk to her cousin Michael, but frankly I don't know if he's any good. As you know I'm unemployed, so maybe he'll give me a discount, but I don't want a price break if it's going to land me in jail with bad advice."

"What's his full name."

"Michael Kosaka."

"And he practices here in L.A.?"

"Yes."

"Give me some time. I'll call you back with some information."

"I was just about to leave the office."

"It will only take me a minute. Just wait."

I gave Mary the office number and rang off. I had time to put my notes on the club mystery back in order when the phone rang. It was Mary.

"Michael Kosaka is an excellent attorney," Mary reported. "My sources say you should get good advice from him."

"Thanks, Mary, I appreciate it."

"So you're not going to explain what's going on?"

"Not right now. I'll tell you as soon as I can."

"Rats!"

"See you soon." Mary was an information junky, but things were happening so fast I didn't know what information to give her right now. One thing I wasn't going to give her was the fact that I was going to spend my morning checking out strip joints. Look, I'm not lily pure and pristine. I'm not even prudish. But I was embarrassed.

I drove to the first club and, of course, it was closed. In front of the club was a couple of display cases with pictures of the girls, and I stopped to look. They all seemed to have names like Ginger and Kiki and Brandy. I didn't recognize any of them. As I stood in front of the club looking at the pictures, I had the thought that someone like Mrs. Kawashiri would probably drive by and see me, and it made me uncomfortable. Still, this was business of sorts, and I pressed on to the second club.

It had the same setup, with pictures in front, along with its own collection of Brandys (this time spelled Brandee) and Gingers, but I didn't see the woman I was looking for, so I went to the theater.

The Paradise Vineyard is an old converted movie theater on the western edge of downtown Los Angeles. The facade of the theater is weathered, and the once-bright gold, red, and yellow designs on the theater's front are now muted and worn.

The marquee on the front of the theater promises "Girls! Girls! Gi ls!" The missing "R" looked as though it had been gone for a long time. Underneath the triple proclamation of what could be found within was a yellow and black banner with the words "Old Time Burlesque!"

I parked my car and walked to the front of the theater, where I was disappointed to see that there were no pictures of the dancers, just a poster informing me that "Cutie Valentine" and "Yolanda LaHuge" were the featured acts. At least they were plumb out of Gingers and Brandies, even though I had a good idea about what it was about Yolanda that was so huge. Still, without photos, it was impossible to tell if the woman I met was dancing there.

"You know someone here?"

I knew that voice, and it was the worst person I could think of to catch me in front of the theater.

"Hello, Officer Hansen. I don't know anyone here."

"That's Detective Hansen," he said. His eyes were already narrowed in suspicion. "If you don't know anyone here, why are you standing in front of the theater?"

"I was hoping to find some picture in front so I could see if the woman I met in Matsuda's room was a dancer here."

"How did you know to come here?"

"I got a list of strip clubs in downtown L.A. and marked the ones near the hotel on a map. Do you want me to show it to you?"

"Yes."

We walked to my car with my face burning red. "I imagine you're doing something similar," I said, as I showed him my Thomas Brothers map with the clubs marked on them.

"I'm interested in why you're doing this," Hansen said.

"I thought it would be helpful if I found the woman. She could back up my story."

"Or deny it."

I bit my tongue and forced myself to smile at the bastard. "It costs nothing to be polite" was one of my father's favorite sayings. He was wrong, of course. Sometimes it costs a great deal of self-control. "That's always a possibility," I answered, "but if she tells the truth, her story should corroborate mine."

"Mr. Tanaka, I'm going to ask you once to stop getting involved in police affairs," Hansen said. "If we need your help, we will ask for it. You don't have to do things on your own that involve this murder."

"All right," I said as I walked around to get into my car. I was going to tell him that he didn't have to bother checking out the two clubs I had already stopped at, but I decided to let him carry out his own investigation. Yes, I know it's petulant and petty, but I think he would have gone to the other clubs anyway.

I drove back to Little Tokyo and went to the Kawashiri Boutique to talk to Mariko.

"I saw that police detective this afternoon. He caught me standing in front of a strip joint looking for that woman, and I'm sure I'm his number one suspect by now. I want to talk to your cousin Michael as soon as possible."

"Oh, great. My boyfriend the criminal. Did you read the story in the *Times?*" Mariko asked.

"Yeah. It was really interesting. Especially the part about Matsuda originally being a U.S. citizen. The *Times* seemed to know about Matsuda awfully fast. I wonder what else they know? I'd love to get more information."

"I've been thinking," Mariko said. "Mrs. Kawashiri has a customer, a Mrs. Okada, who's always talking about her grandson who's a reporter for the *L.A. Times.* He wasn't the person who wrote today's story, but maybe he can give you more information."

"How would I meet him?"

"By asking Mrs. Kawashiri, of course. You know how this works with Japanese, with all the reciprocal favors. All that *ongiri* stuff. Mrs. Okada owes Mrs. Kawashiri. For some reason Mrs. Kawashiri sees more in you than I do, and I'm sure she'd be glad to help you."

Ongiri is how Japanese keep things in social balance. *On* is a debt of gratitude. *Giri* is a sense of duty. You do me a favor or give me a gift, and I'm now obligated to eventually do you a favor or give a gift of equal value. In fact, if I do too big a favor or buy too big a gift in return, it's a kind of a put-down. The exchange of gifts and favors don't balance themselves out.

In most of Japanese or Japanese-American society you don't write things down about who owes whom favors, but in some rural villages in Japan they actually write down all the help and favors one village member gives to another, and they keep these records for generations. A village member might be expected to help another build a barn because that person's great grandfather got help from the barn-raiser's great grandfather a century before, and that social debt has not been balanced out yet! It can get tedious keeping track of things, even without formal mercantile bookkeeping.

Mariko thought that Mrs. Okada owed Mrs. Kawashiri for past favors, and Mrs. Kawashiri would be willing to help me by calling in some of her chips with Mrs. Okada on my behalf. I, of course, would then be obligated to Mrs. Kawashiri.

"Okay, I'll ask Mrs. Kawashiri if she can set something up," I said. "Are you sure Michael will get back to me?"

"Michael's very good about getting back to people. I'm sure as soon as he has a break he'll call me."

Frustrated, but not seeing much I could do about things on the lawyer front, I went into the shop and asked Mrs. Kawashiri if she could ask Mrs. Okada to set up a meeting with her grandson who worked at the *Times*. Mrs. Kawashiri showed genuine pleasure at the prospect of helping me, and said she'd set something up.

I went into the back room where Mariko was waiting and decided to try something else. "Where's the hatbox with the mysterious package."

"On the shelf behind you. Why?"

"Because I'm going to open it."

Mariko reached behind me and took down a hatbox. "No you're not," she announced. "I'm going to open it!"

She took the package out of the box and set to work. Her small fingers busily worked at tearing away the string and tape that held the package together. I cautioned her, because I wanted to be able to put the package back together more-or-less like I found it. She moderated her enthusiasm, but within a few seconds the package was open and lying in her lap was a stack of pale yellow sheets.

"What are they?" I asked.

Mariko picked one up and looked at it. She frowned. "This one seems to be a warranty claim for a TV."

O ne hundred twenty-three thousand, seven hundred three dollars, and sixty-two cents. Did you double-check the total?"

Mariko shook her credit card calculator at me. "Are you saying my machine can't add?"

"I'm saying you might have pressed the wrong key."

"I double-checked it."

"That's an awful lot of money for warranty claims."

"It's weird."

"What's weird?"

"Why all this fuss over a bunch of claim forms?"

Mrs. Kawashiri came into the back room and asked, "Ken-san, can you meet Mrs. Okada right after lunch today? She lives in Culver City and says her grandson can stop by at that time."

"Sure. Can you get me the address?"

Mrs. Kawashiri handed me a piece of paper with Mrs. Okada's address written on it. She looked at the claim forms and said, "What are those?"

I sighed. "That's a good question." I picked up one of the claim forms and looked at it. "I don't know," I confessed. "There is one thing unusual about them, though."

"What's that?" Mariko asked.

"Even though there's a dealer number filled in on the form, the name and address of the business that did the repairs has been left blank."

"Everything else seems to be filled in," Mariko said, looking at one of the forms.

Mrs. Kawashiri picked a form up and looked at it. "Mine's got a little sticker on it," she said, pointing to a white label a quarter-inch high and about two inches long. "There's a bar code or something on it. Do all of them have that?"

Mariko flipped through the pile of claims. "Yeah. They all seem to have a sticker. They're all claims against Mihara Electric Company, too. Right?"

I shuffled through the forms. "That's right, but they're for different things: TVs, VCRs, microwave ovens. A lot of them are bulk claims for fixing five or six TVs or VCRs."

The bell that announced a customer entering the boutique went off. Mariko rose to greet the customer, but Mrs. Kawashiri motioned her down and went back into the shop herself.

"What's the biggest claim?" I asked Mariko.

"About thirteen thousand dollars, I guess. Most of them seem to be between four and ten thousand, but there are a couple in here for just a few hundred dollars. Those are the ones that just have one repair listed on the claim."

"Do the bulk claims all list serial numbers?"

"Sure. Here's one. See? Three TVs and here are the serial numbers, two VCRs and here are the serial numbers, four microwave ovens, a TV satellite dish, and a projection TV. Total parts and labor is seventy-eight hundred bucks."

"Do you think this could be evidence of some kind of fraud?" Mariko said.

"What do you mean?"

"Maybe these things show that somebody was cheating Mihara Electric on its U.S. warranty claims, and Newly is trying to get back the evidence or something."

"I don't see how they could show that, because they don't even have a company name. Although . . . I see they all have the same dealer number."

"Maybe you can trace back from that who originally filled out the claim form, but I don't see how they can be evidence of anything." Mariko put down the claim form she had in her hand. "It's beyond me."

The phone rang, saving me from having to admit bafflement, too. It was Mariko's lawyer cousin Michael. After briefly explaining the situation to him, we made an appointment to meet at three-thirty.

"Give me a couple of the claim forms to take with me, and wrap up the rest." I said as I got off the phone.

"Excuse me, do I look like your personal assistant?"

"No, but you look like someone who will assist me if I bribe her with a large bowl of *udon* noodles for lunch."

"With shrimp tempura on top?"

"Yes, with shrimp tempura on top."

"Your packages, Mr. Tanaka, will be rewrapped in approximately two minutes."

After lunch I dropped Mariko off and drove over to the Culver City address for Mrs. Okada given to me by Mrs. Kawashiri.

Naomi Okada was a small woman. I judged that she couldn't be more than 4'9" tall, but osteoporosis had curved her spine till she seemed even tinier. She met me at the door of her modest Culver City home wearing a dark purple dress with thin black stripes. Her face was remarkably free of lines for her age, which I judged to be at least in the late sixties. Her gray hair was neatly pulled back into a bun, and her deep brown eyes had a bright sparkle of intelligence.

"Mrs. Okada?"

"Yes."

"My name's Ken Tanaka. Mrs. Kawashiri said she talked to you about me."

"Oh, Mr. Tanaka. Please come in. My grandson's not here yet."

She stood aside and let me enter the small, neat living room of her house. A comfortable looking flower print couch, a matching chair, and a maple coffee table made it look like a showroom at an Ethan Allen furniture store. On the coffee table was a book and an arrangement of irises. In one corner of the room was a lacquered wood glass doll case, with a Japanese doll in it. Japanese style, the case stood on the floor, instead of up on a table. The doll was dressed in a miniature print kimono. Its painted face looked up at me with solemn dignity.

"I'm sorry to bother you," I said.

"Oh, it's no bother. I'm happy to introduce you to my grandson, Evan."

"Well, I know it's a big inconvenience."

"It's no inconvenience. Please sit down." She indicated the couch. "Would you like some green tea?"

"No, I don't want to bother you or put you out."

"It's absolutely no bother. Why don't you have some tea?"

"Well, if you're sure it's not a bother, I would like some. Thank you."

"Good."

The complicated dance of apology and refusal, offer and denial was carried out in traditional Japanese fashion, and I could see that Mrs. Okada was pleased that I knew my proper role in the elaborate social interplay. It showed I was "raised right."

Mrs. Okada had the tea things ready in the kitchen, and she returned with them on a tray almost immediately. Of course I was expected to accept the tea, despite all the protestations, so she already had it prepared. If I had either accepted too readily or refused she would have been hurt and put out by my lack of manners. On the tray was a spectacular *satsuma* platter with characteristic gold and colored enamel designs. It held Japanese *arare* rice crackers, and it seemed a shame to use such a lovely piece for such plebeian purposes.

"This platter is beautiful," I said, touching the edge of the dish.

"It's a very poor thing," Mrs. Okada said, even though obviously it wasn't.

When all the social preliminaries had been dispensed with, we sat back in our seats. Mrs. Okada sort of perched on her chair with her legs barely touching the ground. Her curved spine forced her to look up to see me, but her face had an expression of expectation.

"My grandson should be here soon," she said.

"Okay. Do you know what he covers for the *Times?*"

"I'm not totally sure. My eyes are bad so I don't read much anymore. I used to love to read, but now I have a hard time. My daughter sometimes reads stories to me that my grandson wrote. They all seem to do with Asian business."

"You must be proud of him."

She waved that thought away with her hand, but I could see she was pleased. Floundering to make polite small talk until her grandson appeared, I noticed that the book on her coffee table bore the picture of a dark mountain jutting out of a high desert landscape. The book was titled *Heart Mountain.* I pointed to the book.

"Is that book about the Heart Mountain Relocation camp?"

"Concentration camp," she corrected. "Relocation camp is what they call it now to make themselves feel better. The book is about it. I was in that camp during the war."

"Oh. It must have been pretty bad."

"It was bad. The only nice part was you could see Heart Mountain. It was beautiful. Sometimes when I look at the cover of this book and I see the picture of Heart Mountain in Wyoming, it makes me think of Mount Fuji in Japan."

"Were you born in Japan?"

"Heavens, no. I was born in Seattle. My father owned a hardware store before the war. I didn't even visit Japan until the 1960s. I always wanted to see Japan, and I realize now I went at the perfect time, before the dollar became worthless!"

"What was Heart Mountain like?"

"It was just a collection of barracks at the foot of a mountain in Wyoming. The summers were unbearably hot, with all kinds of bugs biting at you. The winters were incredibly cold, with icy air coming out of Canada. I was a teenager then, but I still suffered from the cold during the winter. The old people really suffered. We used to joke that the average yearly temperature at Heart Mountain was great. It was the individual daily temperature that was lousy." She poured the tea as she talked. "It seems like a lot of the camps were put in locations where there were extremes in temperature.

"The barracks at Heart Mountain were just little tar paper and rough board things, so they did nothing to stop the cold and they seemed to increase the heat. The lids from tin cans were in great demand because they could be used to patch knotholes. We were in room F of our barracks, which meant we had a little bigger room. Each barrack had six rooms, of three different sizes. The rooms got smaller in size as you approached the middle."

"How big were the barracks?" I asked, interested.

"About sixty feet in total."

"And your entire family lived in just one room in the barracks?"

"Yes. We had these rusty old army cots from the First World War and we strung blankets across on string to give some privacy. Something like a shelf to hold your possessions was actually a luxury. That's because wood was so scarce. Every winter we would scrounge around for wood to burn to keep us warm. But even if you were lucky enough to find enough wood, the little potbelly stoves in the barracks would hardly take the frost out of the air on some cold mornings.

"The first men into the camps actually built most of it. My father was in that bunch, because they figured that if he owned a hardware store he must know all about construction. He told us the first group of men were convinced they were being taken into the wilderness to be shot. The guards on the train were real mean and they made the men sit in the same position for days. Sitting still for days doesn't sound like much punishment, but after a while it can get to be agony if you're not allowed to even stand up and stretch. They could only get up one at a time to go to the bathroom twice a day, on a regular schedule. If you didn't have to go when it was your time, well, too bad. If you had to go at any other time, well, you just had to hold it.

"When they finally got to Heart Mountain, they found a bunch of tar paper and lumber dumped off by the side of the train tracks and they were forced to build the camp. My father said the materials they provided were junk, and a lot of the men didn't know what they were doing. There was hardly a right angle in any barracks in that camp. He said he thought someone was selling the good lumber and such on the black market. I know the chefs at the camp were selling sugar and milk on the black market. It got so bad that the children didn't have milk to drink and there was almost a riot over that."

"I remember they gave us boiled squid and rice for weeks on end. I know squid is supposed to be a delicacy, but to this day I still can't eat it." She picked up her cup of tea, "You remarked on my *satsuma* platter. At the camp we had these cups and plates that were enormously thick and large. They all had 'U.S.Q.M.C.' on the back, and I can remember wondering what kind of company would make porcelain so thick and clumsy. I eventually found out that 'U.S.Q.M.C.' stood for 'U.S. Quartermaster Corps.' The plates were old army plates from World War One." She laughed. It was a light, friendly laugh.

"From the time I was a little girl I loved porcelain. It came from my mother. When they gave us orders to go to camp we could only take what we could carry. Before we left I remember my mother packing her beloved porcelain away in a barrel for storage. A white man was going door-to-door in our neighborhood buying things from Japanese at just pennies on the dollar. When he got to our house he told my mother everything in storage would be confiscated anyway, and that he'd buy the plates for a penny apiece. I can remember my mother walking to the front door of the house with a handful of plates and throwing them on the sidewalk. They hit and shattered into a thousand pieces. She preferred breaking them over selling them to a profiteer. It turned out our things in storage weren't confiscated, but some were stolen. This *satsuma* platter is one thing that survived." She lightly touched the edge of the platter.

"It sounds like a terrible time."

"We actually tried to have what we thought was a normal American life in camp. We had schools and clubs and even a boy scout troop. But it was a hollow kind of life. In the camps the whole family structure disintegrated. That's what I think was sad. The men felt low and helpless. Kids were uprooted and put in a strange environment. The women put up with things they never had to put up with in civilian life."

"Such as?"

"Well, for instance, the toilets had no doors on them. They were just open-faced stalls, with one side open up for everyone to see. The government wouldn't provide materials for doors. It was humiliating. We had pieces of cardboard we would hold in front of us while we did our business. It was things like that. Little indignities that chipped away at the kind of family we had before the war.

"With the adults adrift, the kids ran loose. It was hard to have a normal life. Everything we had been taught about America and justice and democracy all seemed to have no meaning. Most of us were raised to believe in America, and we felt we were Americans. We couldn't understand why we were shipped off to these camps just because Japan, a foreign country, had attacked us. Eventually, family discipline broke down so much that some of the kids formed gangs. Even some of the men got together in gangs. And the prison guards were no better. Some were okay," she corrected, "but like I said, a lot of them stole rations and sold them on the black market. Besides the squid, for awhile we just had rice and peaches to eat, because the meat they provided was rotten. They were selling all the good meat on the black market. The peaches actually turned out to be a bad thing, even though we kids liked them, because some of the men made stills and fermented alcohol from the peaches."

Mrs. Okada looked at me and laughed. "I'm just running on about bad times! Until recently I wouldn't talk about the camps at all and now I can't seem to shut up!"

"Why didn't you talk about the camps?" I asked, puzzled. The reticence to talk about the camp experience was something I had always noticed in Japanese-Americans who were in them. My family was from Hawaii. Although my grandfather lost his fishing boat because they thought all Japanese with boats must be spies, we were relatively untouched. My mother was at Pearl Harbor during the attack, and during the war she worked as a Red Cross volunteer. The experience of the mainland Japanese-Americans was different from Hawaiian Japanese-Americans, and I was frankly curious.

"We were embarrassed and ashamed. It was like being in prison, even though we had done nothing. But you younger people seem more open about it, and it's made it easier to talk about the experience. The apology and redress for the camps from the U.S. government was also something that helped. I recently went to the Japanese American National Museum and looked up my camp records on their computer system. I even sent away to the National Archives and got a copy of my camp file. They had report cards and school records and even some drawings I did in school. It's both sad and interesting that they keep everybody's files after half a century."

The doorbell rang, and I was so interested that I was actually sorry that Mrs. Okada's grandson finally showed up.

When she opened the door I was surprised to see that Mrs. Okada's grandson was well over six feet tall. He was in his late twenties, with spiky black hair atop a face with the same cheekbones as Mrs. Okada. He was dressed in blue jeans and a Levi's work shirt. Despite the way he towered over the diminutive woman, I learned who the boss was inside of two seconds. "You're late," she scolded. "I've been boring Mr. Tanaka with my ramblings while we've waited for you."

"I'm sorry, Grandma," he said, a faint flush of color coming to his cheeks. She grabbed his arm and guided him inside. An elf leading a giant. She brought him over to me and said, "This is my worthless grandson."

He flushed again, but because of the business with the tea, Mrs. Okada knew that I wouldn't believe she was in earnest. Some Japanese downplay the virtues of their children and spouses and are surprised that others take them seriously. Mrs. Okada knew I wouldn't make that mistake.

"Hi, I'm Ken Tanaka," I said, offering my hand.

"I'm Evan Okada," he said as he shook my hand. We each sat at an end of the couch as Mrs. Okada resumed her perch on the chair.

"I understand that you work as a reporter for the *L.A. Times,*" I said.

"Yes, I do," he said with what I thought was a bit of wariness.

"Did you work on the story about the Japanese national who was killed at the Golden Cherry Blossom Hotel?"

"Why do you ask?"

"Because I was probably one of the last people to see him alive."

Evan's interest picked up. "Did you know him?" he asked.

"Not really. The night he was killed was the only time I met him."

"Do you work at the hotel?"

"No. I had business with him."

"What kind of business?"

"I was just picking up a package from him."

"And when did you see him?"

I laughed. "I guess it's in a reporter's nature to ask questions, but I was really hoping that you could provide me with information, not vice versa. You haven't even answered my original question about if you worked on the story."

"Why are you interested in finding out more information?"

"Because I saw him that night, I think I may be a suspect. Frankly, I want to protect myself by learning about the case. I was surprised about how much information the *Times* story had about Matsuda's background, and I wanted to know how you got the information so fast."

"Actually, it's against our policy to discuss sources for stories."

The frustration must have shown on my face because Mrs. Okada interjected. "Now you answer his questions! Mrs. Kawashiri asked me to see if I could help Ken-san. She said it would be a great kindness to her if I did so. She's been very good to me over the years, and I want you to stop being a bad grandson and help him." She shook a small finger at him as she lectured.

In some Japanese families being a "bad" son or grandson is the ultimate chastisement. A reporter's wariness and the policies of the *Los Angeles Times* were no match for Japanese Grandma Power. Evan crumbled.

"I'm sorry I haven't answered your questions," he said. "It's just that a lot of the information was contained in a dossier I obtained from a confidential source. I didn't write the story, but I did contribute some research. My normal beat is Pacific Rim business stuff, so I'm interested in the business activities of the Yakuza and have contacts with law enforcement who share that interest."

"Matsuda was a member of the Yakuza?"

"Actually, I don't know. He was certainly connected with Yakuza companies that are associated with the Sekiguchi-Gummi crime family, but he didn't appear to be an actual member of the Sekiguchi-Gummi. Maybe his background made him a bit of an outcast. In any case, he seemed to operate as a 'fixer,' someone who acts as a go-between on deals, instead of an actual member of the Yakuza."

"I'm a little confused. I thought the Yakuza was Japanese organized crime. He was acting as some kind of business agent for them?"

"The Yakuza is involved in legitimate businesses like pachinko parlors and bars. Like U.S. organized crime, they also get involved in show business. They also have clearly illegal enterprises, too, like drugs or gun smuggling. It's really complicated. A big Yakuza family like the Sekiguchi-Gummi will have company picnics and operate more-or-less openly. It's sort of like some sections of New York where everybody knows who the wise guys are and who the Don is. Knowing those things and proving criminal activity are two different things."

"Do you think Matsuda was killed by the Yakuza?"

Evan paused for a long moment. "I don't know," he said. "What makes me think he might have been is the fact that he was apparently killed by a sword. A sword is a Yakuza weapon."

"How do you mean?"

"Japan has strict gun control laws. Guns are very difficult to get. They're becoming more common now, but until recently crimes involving guns were very rare, so the Yakuza would use swords and knives for hits. They cut up that movie director, Jizo Itami, because they didn't like a movie he made about them. I've even seen TV news videotape of a Yakuza hit man crawling into the window of a house where an informer was hiding. He took a sword in with him and murdered the informer. Then he bragged on camera afterward, holding the bloody sword."

"Was he crazy?"

"No. Just proud of his work and not too concerned about his personal well-being. There's no death penalty in Japan, and if he had any family he knew they'd be well taken care of by his Yakuza bosses. It's all that Japanese nonsense about loyalty to the group taken to its ultimate, perverse conclusion."

I sat back, soaking in what Evan had told me. During the lull in the conversation, Mrs. Okada leaned forward and patted him on the arm, saying, "I'm pleased that you're helping. Do you want some *arare* crackers?"

12

W hen I was done at Mrs. Okada's I decided to stop at my apartment in Silver Lake to kill time until my appointment with Michael. As I drove I had a lot to think about. Evan didn't know much more about Matsuda's Yakuza connection, so the discussion ended soon after his remark about the sword being a Yakuza weapon. Funnily enough, some of the things that Mrs. Okada had told me affected me more than the stuff Evan Okada told me.

It was my first personal conversation with someone about the camp experience, even though most of the older Japanese-Americans I know on the mainland must have been in a camp. Most simply don't talk about it. From the books, I knew the recitation of facts about the camps, but hearing that something like boiled squid had been served ad nauseam made the experience seem more real.

Also from the books, I knew that at the beginning of World War II over one hundred twenty thousand people had been herded into U.S. camps based solely on their Japanese racial background. About two-thirds of them were American citizens, and many of the ones who weren't citizens were actually prevented from becoming citizens by Asian exclusion laws. In 1922 the U.S. Supreme Court ruled that naturalization for citizenship was only open to whites and people of African descent. Since Asians were neither, the Court said it was constitutional to pass laws that prevented them from becoming citizens or even owning land. The last of these laws were on the books until 1952.

J. Edgar Hoover, hardly a liberal, advised against the camps because the FBI couldn't find a single case of disloyal activity in the Japanese-American community. Ironically, Earl Warren, who was then governor of California and later known as a liberal chief justice of the Supreme Court, pushed for the camps. Even the American Civil Liberties Union, despite the protest of a couple of local chapters, supported the camps.

All people of color have a hard time in our country. We'd like to think that isn't so, but unfortunately it is. I think Asians have had an especially tough time in U.S. culture because for over a century an Asian face has been the face of the enemy.

First were the Chinese. The Chinese were imported to the U.S. to build the railroads and to wash the laundry, but they were soon branded as the "Yellow Peril" and viewed with hatred and suspicion when they dared to think that they could share the American dream.

Then came the Filipinos. As a result of our annexing the Philippines as part of the Spanish-American War, we became engaged in a vicious guerrilla war in our newly acquired colony. The fanatic charges of Filipinos caused the U.S. Army to adopt the .45 caliber automatic as the standard handgun, because this pistol had the stopping power to drop a man in his tracks. Some of the things we did in the Philippines at the turn of the century foreshadowed our worst actions in Vietnam.

Then came the Japanese and World War II. The attack on Pearl Harbor was truly an infamous act, but an equally infamous act was herding Japanese-Americans into camps based on the notion that an Asian face meant a traitor's face.

Then came the Korean War, where even the people we were supposed to be helping (the South Koreans) were "gooks" to our troops, just like the North Korean enemy.

Eventually the Southeast Asians got their turn with Vietnam. That war is too close for me to even understand my feelings about it. Like a lot of Americans, I thought the war was wrong. And like a lot of young American men, I still went to war because I couldn't define what courage really meant.

I guess to some people we will never be "real" Americans because our faces remain Asian, even though our hearts belong to the United States. That's a sad fact that gnaws at us. By the time I got home I was depressed. I got more depressed when I played the messages on my machine. Detective Hansen had called. I dialed the number he left.

"This is Police Detective Hansen."

"This is Ken Tanaka. Did you want to speak to me?"

"Yes. I'm wondering if I could ask your cooperation in something."

"Yes?" This was a new development, asking me for help.

"None of the clubs downtown have a dancer that matches your description, but when I went to the Paradise Vineyard they had three redheads dancing there. None of them would admit to knowing Mr. Matsuda, so I'd like you to go down there this evening before their first show to see if you can identify the woman you saw with Mr. Matsuda two nights ago."

"What time?"

"Five o'clock."

"Can you make it five-thirty?" I didn't want to cut my appointment with Michael at three-thirty short. His office was in the mid-Wilshire district and the traffic might be a problem.

"Okay."

"Can you pick me up in front of the office building where you first met me?"

"Sure."

"Okay, I'll see you then. Good-bye."

I hung up the phone. The police not finding the woman who was with Matsuda was not a good sign.

Michael's office was in one of the glass cube office buildings that dot Los Angeles. I suppose the first one of these had some style, but now there're so many of them that they sort of blend into the horizon. After going through the preliminaries with the receptionist, I was ushered into Michael Kosaka's domain.

Michael had a raffish beard that made him look like a pirate, an image that isn't totally inappropriate for a single practice attorney. From the gray in his hair I'd say he was in his early forties, and he had a hint of a middle-aged paunch gently pressing against the belly of his light blue shirt.

His office was decorated in highly polished rosewood furniture, and on his walls he had Japanese *Ukiyo-e* woodblock prints. Two were Hiroshiges, and another was a triptych of Yoshitoshi's flute player: expensive antiques.

Japanese woodblocks are interesting. In the 1700s and 1800s they were made to be sold for literally pennies. That's why there are series of woodblocks like "100 Views of the Moon" or "100 Views of Edo (Tokyo)." The artist wanted you to collect all one hundred so he could turn a reasonable profit on things that sold so cheaply. Now a masterpiece by a Hokusai or a Hiroshige, which originally sold for pennies, can fetch enormous sums of money. Something inexpensive and new eventually turns into something expensive and old. It's a kind of alchemy.

To make a woodblock, individual cherry wood blocks are carved for each color in the print. The blue color has its own block, the red its own block, and so forth. When a piece of mulberry paper is printed with all the blocks, the image emerges. All the blocks have to be in perfect alignment, or register, for the picture to come out clearly. Sometimes when you see a block for just one color, it's hard to see what the picture is. It occurred to me that unraveling crimes is a little like woodblock printing. Layer after layer is put together until the total picture emerges, and everything has to fit together properly if the picture is going to look clear.

The L.A. County Museum of Art has an example of the same Yoshitoshi flute player that I saw on Michael's wall. It's a three-panel print of a flute player walking across a marshy plain under a full moon. Behind some marsh grass a robber waits to attack the traveler and kill him. As I recall the legend, the music of the flute so enchanted the robber that he let the traveler go. The example in the museum's collection is pretty ratty and soiled, but Kosaka's example was in excellent condition, with still-vibrant colors. I decided the first thing I better talk about was his fee. The office, furniture, and especially the art all spelled money.

After the usual hellos, I said, "Did Mariko explain my financial condition to you?"

Kosaka laughed. "She said if I charge you more than two hundred fifty dollars, I'll have to sit at the kiddies table the next time the family gets together for Thanksgiving."

I smiled both at the threat and the fact that I could swing $250, even though it was probably what Michael got per hour. "That I can handle financially," I confirmed, and I launched into my story about Rita Newly, Matsuda, and my gaff about the package. Kosaka sat there listening to me intently, occasionally making notes on a pad of paper with a very elegant gold fountain pen and nodding his head or making encouraging murmurings.

When I was done he sat back in his chair for a moment and thought. "Where's this package?" he asked.

"Actually, Mariko has it where she works."

Michael thought a little more. Then he leaned across the desk and said to me, "It's easy to understand how anyone could get confused after several hours of questioning, especially about such a horrible crime. Is that why you misspoke about what happened to the package?" He looked at me and raised one eyebrow. Well, I don't need a ton of bricks to hit me. I said, "Yes, I just got confused."

He leaned back into his chair, pleased. "Of course. Very understandable. And at the first opportunity, you're going to march in and correct your mistake."

I checked my watch. "That could be in seventy minutes or so. That detective wanted me to go with him to a theater to identify the woman I saw at the hotel."

Kosaka pursed his lips. "If he asks you about the package again, you'll of course tell the truth and explain you got confused. But if he doesn't ask you, I think tomorrow will be soon enough to correct your mistake. Let me call a friend of mine in the D.A.'s office to ask, in a general way, the best approach to correcting your mistake. That may take a day or two if my friend's not in the office. This detective may not be the best person to go to with your correction. So just sit tight for a couple of days until I contact you."

"Okay, I'll wait for your call before doing anything else."

"And Ken . . ."

"Yes?"

"This is really none of my business, but you might also think about stopping this adventuring. That detective sounds like a jerk, but he is right about your meddling. This is a brutal murder case, and whoever did it may not like an amateur poking his nose in. That obviously goes for the police, as well."

That was good advice. I wish I had heeded it.

Hansen was about ten minutes late when he picked me up at the office to go to the Paradise Vineyard. He was driving a big green American sedan . . . what passes for an unmarked police car for the LAPD. The drive from the office to the Paradise Vineyard Theater took about twenty minutes in downtown traffic, so I decided to make small talk.

"Have you been in Los Angeles long?"

"Eleven years," Hansen said. He didn't volunteer more.

"Where are you originally from?"

"Walnut Creek."

"Up by San Francisco?"

"Yeah."

"How did you get involved in police work."

"My first choice didn't work out."

"What was that?"

"Professional football."

"Really? What college did you play for?"

"San Jose State."

"What position?"

"Linebacker."

"Did you go directly from college to the Police Academy?"

"First I was in the marines."

"So how did you get involved in police work?"

"My uncle was the police chief of Walnut Creek."

"And he got you involved?"

"Yeah."

It was not a stimulating conversation. I thought about working in my army record in the conversation to show I could be macho, too, and I immediately felt shame. Why was I was seeking approval from someone that I shouldn't need approval from?

I have a Bronze Star and Purple Heart from Vietnam, but they were earned in what I think is a truly embarrassing way. Three weeks after I arrived in Vietnam my squad became engaged in a fire fight. My squad leader told me to make my way down a steep ravine to see if I could flank the enemy and engage him in enfilade fire. As I made my way down the side of the ravine I didn't realize how steep it was, and I slipped and fell to the bottom. I hit right on my tailbone. I heard a sickening, crunching sound, and the world around me literally started turning black. The sound of gunfire up the hill from me was muted by a red fog of pain and a need to vomit.

I don't know if I actually blacked out, but I do know that when I tried to move a few minutes later, the pain in my spine was so intense it literally took my breath away. Now comes the really stupid part. Instead of lying down and obeying my body, I continued down the ravine and to the side of the enemy. I managed to flank the enemy and I started firing. To be honest, I was in so much pain that I didn't even aim. I just shot in the general direction and made a lot of noise.

It worked. The enemy withdrew, and several hours later they got me to a field hospital. I walked into the hospital on my own, and they immediately took X rays. I remember the look on the doctor's face as he got on a field telephone to talk to a specialist someplace. I didn't hear the whole conversation, but I do remember the doctor saying, "I can't believe this guy walked in here on his own. He's lucky he's not paralyzed." That scared me. A lot.

I had crushed my second lumbar vertebra, and the splintered bones could have severed my spinal cord and paralyzed me permanently. Instead the result was seven months in a body cast, a Bronze Star, and a Purple Heart. I figure I got both for literally busting my ass and not having enough sense to realize it. I had spent less than a month in Vietnam.

I seldom talk about the experience because I still find it silly and disturbing. And I never go to veteran reunions and similar events, because I feel that with my Asian face I'm looked at as the enemy, not a comrade. One positive effect of my being at these events is that the number of "slope" stories get curtailed, but this effect is not worth the discomfort.

Now I was going to talk about this experience with a stranger I didn't much like, just because I was insecure about my own manhood. We're funny and sometimes lamentable creatures. I quit talking, and we covered the rest of the way to the theater in silence.

13

Hansen pulled around the side of the Paradise Vineyard Theater and stopped his car in an alleyway in a no parking zone. He got out of the car and I followed him up to a metal-clad door with a faded NO ADMITTANCE stenciled on it.

Without bothering to knock, Hansen turned the door handle and entered the theater with me in tow. I'm not used to being backstage in theaters, and I was surprised at how tall the ceiling was. It went up into a seemingly endless darkness, and high in the rafters I could see catwalks, backdrops, and a spider's skein of ropes. The air in the theater had a musty, stale odor that left a metallic taste in my mouth.

Near the door a laconic, fat stagehand was sitting on a chair and smoking a cigarette. The stagehand wore a short, blue T-shirt that didn't hide the rolling flesh of his belly. Between the bottom of the T-shirt and the top of his blue jeans was a round tube of pale flesh that sprouted curly brown hairs. On the front of the T-shirt was the message "Stud for Hire" in white letters. I believe in the power of advertising, but I don't believe this guy got any business from the shirt.

"Where's the manager?" Hansen demanded.

The stagehand watched us with his small dark eyes, then he pointed to the back edges of the stage with a hand that held the half-smoked cigarette.

Hansen marched off in the general direction indicated, and I scurried after him. Behind the backdrop of the curtain was an open area that seemed set aside for practice.

Sitting on a chair in this practice area was a small Asian man. His hair was a streaked salt and pepper, combed straight back. Around his neck was a pale blue silk scarf that tucked into a finely cut dark blue shirt. He wore dark blue slacks and white shoes. Resting across his lap was a black cane with a silver handle, and draped over the back of the seat was a large black overcoat, two very unusual accessories for Los Angeles.

The man was talking softly to a woman dressed in gray leotards and leg warmers. He was giving direction in a calm, authoritative voice, with the woman listening intently and nodding her head on occasion. The woman appeared to be in her late twenties, and I thought that she was surprisingly attractive.

"Yoshida?" Hansen called as he walked across the practice area toward the man in the chair.

He turned his head and fixed Hansen with his gaze. Dark, bushy eyebrows capped the man's intense eyes. By his face, I judged the man to be in his sixties, but he could have been older. He was in good shape, so it was hard to tell. Deep lines etched his face, and his jaw tightened as he recognized Hansen. I knew the feeling.

He turned and said a few words to the woman, who gave Hansen and me a sour look as she walked out of the practice area and back toward the darkness of the theater.

"Officer Hansen," the man said. His tone was flat and emotionless.

"Mr. Yoshida, this is Mr. Tanaka." Hansen pointed at me. "As I told you on the phone, I brought him along to see if he can identify the lady who was with Matsuda."

Yoshida's eyes slipped past Hansen and locked onto me. I felt myself dissected by the two hard orbs. My clothes, my looks, and perhaps even my history were being absorbed, categorized, and filed by the hard eyes of Yoshida. He gave no word of greeting; instead he nodded. "I'll go and get the girls," he said.

As he got out of the chair, I noted that he leaned heavily on the cane, and I watched with fascination as the small Japanese limped to the back of the theater using the cane to carry part of his weight on every step.

"Who's Yoshida?" I asked.

"He's the stage manager at the theater," Hansen responded. "He sort of runs things backstage, and he also coaches the girls in their routines. The guys at the station tell me he's been doing it for years."

Yoshida hobbled back into the practice area with two women following him. One was a Latina with a tall pile of red hair. The crimson of her lipstick made a large slash across her mouth which was picked up by the red dress she was wearing. The second woman had pale white skin and short red hair. She had a short, white terry cloth robe on and her hands were thrust in the robe's pockets.

"This is Miss Rosie Martinez," Yoshida said, "who dances under the name of the Mexican Firecracker, and this is Mrs. Valerie Welsh, who is known as Cutie Valentine." He looked at me, as if expecting me to acknowledge acquaintance with one of the two women.

"Neither one of these ladies is the one I saw with Matsuda," I said.

"Where's the third woman?" Hansen asked.

"What are you talking about?"

"When I was here before there were three redheads. Now there are only two. What happened to the third one?"

"Ah. That's Miss Sanchez. I'm afraid she left and hasn't returned yet. She said she was ill."

"When will she be back?"

Yoshida shrugged. "Who knows. The girls can sometimes be very unreliable. She didn't call to tell me if she'll be here for tonight's show. I have no idea when she'll be in."

"I took her phone number and address," Hansen said. "Can I borrow your phone? I'd like to call her and see if she's home."

Without answering, Yoshida hobbled off the stage and Hansen trailed after him. The two women started to leave.

"Excuse me a second," I said.

The women looked at me quizzically.

"Could you answer a few questions for me?"

A look of suspicion flashed across Welsh's face, and Martinez crossed her arms and shifted her weight onto one foot. Talk about body language.

"I'm not a cop," I added. "So you really don't have to answer any questions if you don't want. I'm just a guy that's caught up in this, and maybe the other lady is, too. Her name's Sanchez?"

"Angela. Angela Sanchez," Martinez said.

I focused my attention on her. "Is she really sick?"

She shrugged.

"I'm just asking because she might be in something that she really doesn't want to be involved in. I know that's my feeling. I saw the murdered guy on business the other night and now I'm traipsing around with this cop. I'd much rather be doing something else. Like I said, maybe Angela's involved the same way."

Martinez shrugged again.

"Can I ask you if she was with the Japanese gentleman who was murdered?"

Martinez looked at me, sizing me up. "You can ask," she said.

"I'm leaving," the pale girl announced, and turned around and walked out of the area. As Martinez also turned to leave, I touched her on the arm and said, "Please don't go. I really need your help."

"Ask Fred. I don't know nothing," the girl said.

"Who's Fred?"

"Yoshida."

"Oh. Okay. Thanks."

Hansen came back with Yoshida a few minutes later.

"Nobody's home," Hansen remarked.

"Maybe she's on the way," Yoshida said. "She tends to keep her own hours, anyway. I have no idea when she'll be back"

"Yeah. Right."

I suppressed a giggle. It occurred to me that Detective Hansen sometimes talked like Jack Webb on the old *Dragnet* TV series. Maybe there was a course on talking like that at the L.A. Police Academy.

Hansen took me back to the office, and I went to pick Mariko up so we could have a quick dinner and drive out to the valley for her AA meeting.

I've never seen Mariko drunk. And sometimes I don't understand why she has to go to AA meetings three or four times a week. Based on Mariko's urging, I had educated myself a little bit about alcoholism. Contrary to what I used to think, most alcoholics aren't sleeping in gutters. Since alcoholism is a progressive disease, they might end up that way, but for the most part alcoholics are able to hold down jobs and can even have successful careers. Mariko was able to keep a good job with a bank, but she couldn't control her drinking, especially on weekends. For a good part of her life, she didn't want to control her drinking.

Now a good part of her life was dominated by her desire to not drink. And tonight I was sitting on a folding chair in an effort to support her.

"This is hard," she said. Mariko stood in front of fifty people at the Alcoholics Anonymous meeting in the San Fernando Valley. It was her first time as a speaker and it was at a meeting that wasn't one of the ones she normally attended. Since it was an open meeting that anyone could attend, she asked me to go along for support. Even though we had both been puzzled by the stack of invoices in the package, and equally surprised at the disappearance of Angela Sanchez, the details of life continue. Mariko's first time speaking at an AA meeting was important, and I wanted to be there.

"My name is Mariko and I'm an alcoholic."

"Hi, Mariko," the crowd said in unison, in AA fashion.

"This is my first time as a speaker and I thought it might be easier at a meeting I don't normally attend. But as I look out at you I'm frankly glad to see at least one face I know." She smiled at me.

"What's strange about me being intimidated by a new group of people is that I want to be an actress and I've never in my life had stage fright. Yet, as I stand here, I have all the classic symptoms. I have sweating palms, a churning stomach, vertigo, and the fear that I'll just clam up and not produce more than a croak, instead of words. I've been told that's what stage fright is. Of course, maybe I just ate a bad burrito for dinner."

The crowd laughed, which seemed to give Mariko confidence.

"When I'm on stage I'm usually playing someone else. It's easy to play someone else, but I think everyone in AA has learned that it's hard to play yourself. Scratch that, it's hard to *be* yourself.

"I think that's one reason I started drinking. When I was drunk it was easy to be someone else and not face my own feelings and problems. I grew up in Columbus, Ohio, and my father was a professor at Ohio State. If you look at my face, it's easy to see that I don't fit the mold of what you'd call your typical midwestern farm girl. I'm Japanese and for awhile I thought I was the only Japanese in Ohio. I wish I had a dollar for everyone who told me how good my English was when I was growing up, but I don't speak Japanese, or any other foreign language, for that matter. It was just hard to be so different.

"That raised a lot of issues that I'm still working out, but I found that in the small world of a college town it was easier to be accepted if you drank like a fish. I guess it's the same thing these days, and many of you in this room probably had your drinking problem start in high school or college, when drinking was cool and something everyone did.

"Maybe it was something everyone did, but when I did it I was different. I was an alcoholic, and no matter how many times I convinced myself that I could stop anytime I wanted, I found that I couldn't, at least not without the help of AA.

"I got married right out of college. Naturally, to another alcoholic. At the time I didn't know he was an alcoholic. I just thought he was a fun guy.

"Did I mention that my husband was a Caucasian? No? Well, most Japanese-Americans actually marry outside their race, so either we're totally assimilated and not racially sensitive, or there's something about other races that attracts us. Either way, in a few generations there may no longer be any pure Japanese-Americans, except for the new Japanese who come from Japan as immigrants.

"Well, I realize now that the fact that my ex-husband was Caucasian had a lot to do with me marrying him. The only Japanese boys I knew were nerdy foreign exchange students, so my image of Japanese men wasn't good. I was so insecure in my own racial and personal identity that having a Caucasian husband was important to me. I just didn't realize it at the time. I know I say that a lot, but it's funny how much you do start to realize when you join AA and follow the program. It's like you spend a good part of your life in a fog, and the discipline of the program forces you to penetrate the fog in an effort to see clearly.

"My husband was a lot of fun when I first met him. He got drunk. I got drunk. We got drunk together. When I was still at the stage where getting drunk was fun, it seemed like a great idea to marry Kurt. When I got to the point where the alcohol was starting to kill me, the getting drunk together ceased to be fun. When I tried to stop, it just added to the misery. He got defensive and abusive, and I got a little crazy. He started turning mean when he was drunk. I was going to Alcoholics Anonymous meetings to work on my drinking and also going to Al-Anon meetings because my spouse was a drunk. In the vernacular of AA that made me a double winner. Kurt hadn't hit bottom, and I had. I knew that if I didn't get my drinking under control I'd never get a chance to try acting. I had to get out.

"Now I've been sober for almost four years. When I was a drunk I had a job I hated, but which paid well. Now I'm a starving actress. When I was a drunk I had a marriage that I found meaningless, but it provided a comfortable and mindless kind of security. Now I have an unemployed boyfriend who I sometimes think is crazy, even though I'm madly in love with him. When I was a drunk it was important to me to have a husband who was a Caucasian. Now it's almost an accident that my boyfriend is Japanese, and I frankly wouldn't care what race he was. When I was a drunk I had a lot of unresolved issues about being Japanese in a white society, and although I at least now realize I have all these issues, they're still not resolved. I mention all this to illustrate that when you get sober, your life doesn't immediately become peaches and cream. And if it does, you may not like peaches and cream."

She checked her watch. "Well, once I got started I ran way over the five minutes they wanted me to speak. Since this was my first time up here, they were trying to be easy on me and not give me too much time to fill. I guess they didn't really know me. There's a lot more I could say about myself and what AA has done for me, but I guess the one thing I want to leave you with is the message that a sober life is not always a life without struggle and problems, but it is a life worth living because you will find the courage to be yourself, instead of an alcohol-induced stranger. Thanks."

Mariko walked through the audience and sat next to me. The crowd gave her enthusiastic applause, and I was surprised to feel that she was actually trembling when she sat down. I gave her a hug, and we settled in to listen to the next speaker.

On the way to my apartment after the meeting, we stopped and bought some ice cream as a kind of celebration. We ate banana splits and I told her about the meeting at the Paradise Vineyard that afternoon. Then I said, "Do you know you're one of my heroes?"

Mariko seemed flustered. "What do you mean?"

"I admire the way you've reinvented yourself."

"I'm sick. I have no choice if I want to live."

"You have choices. You could stay the way you were. Most people do. Changing yourself is the hardest thing in the world. It takes courage. I wish I had the same courage."

"You've never had a drinking problem."

"Yeah, but I have life problems. Or maybe midlife problems. I haven't been very active looking for a new programming job. I used to enjoy the work, but now I feel like I'm drifting. I wish I had the courage to just strike out and do what I want to."

Mariko sighed. "I'm torn between encouraging you to get a programming job that will pay you a salary that will allow you to entertain me in a style better than Baskin-Robbins, or encouraging you to follow your dream. What is it you want to do?"

"That's just the problem. I don't know. That's why I feel like I'm past forty and drifting."

She put her hand on mine. It was slightly sticky from the ice cream. She smiled. "Well, we can drift along together. Remember, one day at a time."

I checked my watch and said, "We can't drift along too much tonight. We better finish up. I want to do some more work."

"What?" Mariko said. "It's almost midnight. What kind of

work could you possibly be doing this late?"

"I'm going to go back and glean the field, to see if there's something I've missed. I'm returning to the Paradise Vineyard and see if I can find the girl who was in Matsuda's room."

"Why do you want to see a bunch of floozies?"

"I don't want to see the strippers," I answered. "I want to see the stage manager."

After dropping Mariko off at her apartment I drove downtown and pulled up to the back of the Paradise Vineyard. I didn't have the gall to park in the no parking zone in the alley like Hansen, so I parked about half a block away. I checked my watch before leaving the car. It was twenty after twelve.

I went to the stage door entrance of the theater and walked in. As before, the door was unlocked and no one challenged me as I entered the theater. From the stage loud music was being projected to the audience, but backstage it had an oddly hollow sound to it.

I saw Yoshida standing in the wings, talking to a woman wearing a flowing white blouse and a short black skirt. Incongruously, the woman was holding an electric fan in one hand.

The music ended to a scattering of applause and a few whistles. The applause continued for a few minutes and died, then a bare-breasted woman wearing a G-string came off stage. In her hand she was clutching some blue satin cloth. The woman was Martinez, but if she recognized me she didn't give any indication of it as she passed. In fact, she gave no indication that I was alive at all. I could have been a stage prop. So much for my animal magnetism.

Slow, languid music started up from the speakers, and the woman with the fan walked onto the stage amidst applause and a few hoots from the audience.

Martinez headed backstage to where the dressing rooms were.

She seemed totally at ease and not the least bit caring that she was almost completely nude.

I walked up to Yoshida, who was leaning heavily on his cane. On stage, I could see the woman had plugged the fan into a socket inset in the floor of the stage. Now she was standing before the fan, letting the breeze catch her hair, whipping it back, as she stroked her neck and slowly moved her hips in rhythm with the music.

"Mr. Yoshida?"

Yoshida glanced at me. "The cop," he said. "Angela Sanchez never showed up. I already told your buddy that when he called earlier tonight."

"I'm not a policeman," I corrected.

Yoshida absorbed that information and said, "What do you want?"

"I'd like to talk to you."

"What about?"

"I think you can help me."

"Help you with what?"

"That's what I wanted to talk to you about. Look," I said. "Is there any place we can talk, where it's not so loud?"

The booming music from speakers echoed over our heads, radiating out to the audience. I looked past the stage at the audience. There were twenty-five or thirty patrons in the theater, all men. Most seemed to be older, although there did seem to be a couple of younger ones in the audience. Several were surprisingly well-groomed.

On stage, the girl had untucked the blouse from her skirt and was letting it billow in the breeze of the electric fan.

"She's the last act," Yoshida said. "If you'll buy me a beer, I'll talk to you. But after the act I have to come back and lock up."

"Okay," I readily agreed.

Yoshida nodded and started hobbling off toward the stage door, leaning heavily on the silver-handled cane. By the stage door, Yoshida stopped and pulled on a black overcoat hanging on a hook by the door. He knotted the coat's belt around his waist. With the cane, he actually looked quite dapper.

"Okay," Yoshida said. "There's a bar just down the block. We can talk there."

I followed Yoshida out through the stage door and down the alley to the bar. The bar had a well-worn feeling to it, and it might have passed as a neighborhood joint if it wasn't for the hookers and drug dealers standing in front of it. Of course, in downtown L.A. maybe that's what constituted a neighborhood bar.

At the bar Yoshida eased himself into a booth. He placed the cane across his knees and studied me with interest. "You're Japanese, too," he said, as if it was some kind of discovery.

"Yes. My name's Tanaka, Ken Tanaka."

"I remember. What is it you want me to help you with?"

"I'm interested in finding Angela Sanchez. I think she's probably the woman who was with the guy killed at the Golden Cherry Blossom Hotel."

Yoshida shrugged. "I don't know where she is."

"You must have some idea," I said. "You have her home address."

"I already gave that to the police."

"I'm not the police. And I got the impression that the dancers trusted and respected you."

I could see that Yoshida was pleased by this, in spite of himself.

"I help them with their routines, their dancing skills, and polish up their acts," Yoshida said.

It had never occurred to me that strippers needed dancing skills or a polished act, and the expression on my face must have mirrored my thoughts.

"I know it's a dirty job, but it's all I can get," Yoshida said. "In Japan my ancestors were farmers. They made a living pushing dirt and hauling around human crap to fertilize it. That wasn't a pleasant job, either, but they seemed to do it with dignity and some measure of pride. I've got a job where I push around the dirt of humanity, too, and I still try to do it with some measure of pride and dignity. Did you ever go to a topless bar? The kind where they have dancers?"

"Once, when I was in the army," I said. "I don't like being exploited, and I figured that the whole game was exploitation of one sort or another, so I never went back."

"Did you see the dancers there?"

I nodded.

"What did you think?"

"Some were pretty, most were sad."

Yoshida snorted in exasperation. "No, I mean what did you think of the dancing?"

"It was just dancing. I remember the music was too loud and hurt your ears, but that's about it."

"That's what I mean," Yoshida said, "nothing there was memorable. Some naked amateur gets up wiggles her rear. That's supposed to be exciting? It's supposed to be sensuous? Unless you've got the mind of a smutty fourteen-year-old, it's not even interesting. Now, with my girls down at the Paradise Vineyard, it's different. There's always a reason for them to do what they're doing. Let's say it's hot. A girl comes on stage with an electric fan. She's dressed in a flowing blouse and a skirt. She puts the fan on the floor and stands in front of it. The skirt is whipped up, showing her legs. She uses her hands to cup the breeze and divert it to her face.

"Already you're kind of interested, intrigued to see what's going to go on next. The skirt whipping up reminds you of Marilyn Monroe standing on that grating in *The Seven Year Itch,* and the flash of skin teases you about what's to come. The music starts to play softly, and because it's so hot, the girl starts to remove her blouse, swaying gently to the music. As she removes each garment, the breeze from the fan catches the cloth, alternately hiding and exposing the girl's body to the audience. She drops each garment to the ground, and the whole audience is mesmerized, waiting to see what she's going to do next." Yoshida sat back and slowly twirled his glass of beer between his fingers.

"That's the kind of thing I do," he said. "I provide the brain power to make the bodies on stage interesting. It's not doing a big-time musical, but it is making use of some of my talents in a back water of show business."

"Have you ever tried getting work elsewhere?" I asked.

"A couple of times. It's hard for a crippled choreographer to get work. And I had another problem. You see this face?" Yoshida pointed to himself. "An Asian face is what you find on most of the people in the world. Here, it's a handicap. Even before my accident, it was a problem getting work as a dancer. When I was a kid, I thought I was going to be the next Fred Astaire. I had the moves, I had the style, I had the dance steps, and I even had a better singing voice than Astaire . . . 'I'm putting on my top hat . . .'"

Yoshida sang the first line of the Astaire classic in a surprisingly clear tenor voice.

"I used to bug my mother to spend the money she earned selling produce from her vegetable garden on dancing lessons for me. I used to work on learning dance steps until I was close to collapse. Then I'd catch my breath, get up, and start working some more. I was a fanatic at it because I thought I'd become the greatest song and dance man in the world. It took some hard knocks in life to convince me otherwise."

As I sat nursing my beer, I was struck by how dapper Yoshida was. It wasn't so much that his clothes were fastidious or that his hair was meticulously in place, but how he sat and moved. He had stage presence. At one time it was obvious that he had been trained to cultivate that presence and to project it to the audience, even if it was only an audience of one.

"It's a shame you weren't allowed a chance to try your skills as a singer and dancer," I said.

Yoshida looked at me and tilted his head slightly, acknowledging the sympathy. "I say the fact that I was Japanese was a barrier because it was," Yoshida said. "But actually what killed all hope was this." He slapped his left leg.

"What happened?" I asked, and almost immediately regretted asking, because I was sure that Yoshida had been asked that question a million times before.

"World War Two."

"Oh?"

"That's right, but perhaps not what you think. Like most of the rest of the West Coast Japanese, I was sent to a camp. Man, it was cold there."

I remembered what Mrs. Okada said and asked, "Were you at Heart Mountain?"

Yoshida looked startled and said "No. Manzanar. Why do you ask?"

"I just talked to someone who was at Heart Mountain today and she remarked about how cold it was there. That's why I thought you might have been at Heart Mountain. Wasn't Manzanar in the desert?"

"Yes, but during the winter it could get awfully cold, too. That's why when the opportunity came for me to volunteer to go into the army, leaving the camp didn't sound so bad."

"Were you in the 442nd?" I asked, referring to the famous all-Japanese combat team, the most decorated in the U.S. Army.

"I was supposed to be in the 442nd, but I never made it. I never made it past two weeks in boot camp. They were supposed to be teaching us to throw hand grenades, but some of our guys really weren't very coordinated. We were throwing them from these bunkers, really just a pile of sandbags in a U-shape. One of the guys pulled the pin on a grenade and threw it, but it didn't go very far. It just sort of hit the ground and sat there. We were all ducked down behind, but nothing happened, so we decided the grenade was a dud.

"The guy who was training us, a staff sergeant, really wasn't very smart. He was a big Southern boy and I figured he was given us bunch of Japanese to train as some kind of punishment. I don't think he was malicious, but like I said, I don't think he was very smart. Instead of evacuating all of us straight back from behind the bunker, after about ten minutes he told us to go over to the next bunker.

"I had just left the safety of the sandbags when the grenade went off. The guy who tossed it barely tossed it out onto the range. It was a pathetic throw really. It was more dangerous to us than it would have been to any enemy.

"Anyway, it went off and I caught a bunch of shrapnel in my leg and hip. That wouldn't have been so bad, but it cut a bunch of tendons instead of just embedding itself in the fleshy part of the leg.

"If the guy who threw the grenade had just been a little bit more coordinated, it wouldn't have been close enough to do me any damage. Or if the sergeant in charge of our group had shown a little bit more patience, or had been a little bit smarter in the way he evacuated us, I wouldn't have been hit, either. In fact, I've often thought that just a few seconds delay in leaving the shelter of the sandbags would have saved me."

He smiled and said, "Well, it can't be helped. That's what killed my dancing and my military career. I never got overseas. I never got to try professional dancing, although I think now maybe that would have been butting my head against a wall. Being a Japanese song and dance man right after World War Two wouldn't have been easy."

"We sort of have something in common. I was in Vietnam only three weeks when I got a back injury. Did they send you back to the camp after you recovered?"

"Oh, yes. Manzanar was my home for the duration."

"Look, Mr. Yoshida, maybe you can help me find Angela."

"What's your interest in her?"

"She can help me establish the time when I visited Matsuda."

"Are you a suspect?"

"I don't know, but I don't think so," I said. "At least not yet. But I did see Matsuda that night and the only one who can really establish when I saw him is Angela Sanchez. I've developed a real interest in this case for other reasons, and I want to speak to her."

Yoshida looked at me for a few long moments. I could see the aloofness, which had started to flee while Yoshida told his story of the hand grenade, returning. "I can give you her home address and telephone number when we get back to the theater, but I really can't do much else."

After getting the information I drove back to my apartment in Silver Lake. I was surprised to see Mariko curled up on my couch with a blanket pulled over her. She knew where I hid my extra key, and she had driven over from her own apartment and let herself in. I walked over to the edge of the couch, put my hand on her shoulder, and leaned forward and kissed her.

"How were the strippers?" she said. Her eyes were closed, but her voice was wide awake.

"I told you I went there for business," I protested.

"Monkey business," she said, her eyes popping open. Her face was serious, but I could see a playful gleam in her eyes.

"Well, I really went there to talk to the stage manager and choreographer, a guy called Yoshida."

"Aha. And you didn't see any naked girls?"

"Well, one," I admitted, "but only because she strutted past me going offstage."

"And I suppose you modestly closed your eyes when she did so?"

"Well, it was really hard to close them. They were bulging out."

Mariko twisted around and playfully started to punch me. I grabbed her arms and soon we were involved in an impromptu wrestling match. Within minutes the wrestling match turned into something quite different.

Mariko fell asleep after our lovemaking, but as I got under the covers and snuggled up to her, I kept thinking about what Yoshida had told me. I also thought about Mariko and her struggles as an actress and an alcoholic. I thought about her standing up in front of a group of strangers to share part of her story in an effort to make it easier for others who were taking the same journey she was. I buried my face into the fragrance of Mariko's hair and felt very protective toward her.

The next morning Mariko took off for work and I tried calling Angela Sanchez. The phone rang for a long time before it was answered.

"*Habla.*" A man's voice: Latino, gruff, and sounding a bit older.

"I'd like to speak to Angela Sanchez, please."

"Who the hell are you?" Anger and heavily accented English.

Surprised, I said, "I beg your pardon? I'd just like to speak to Miss Sanchez."

"Angela is my *mujer*. Why are you calling her? She's not here. Who are you?" Real anger now. The man was almost shouting.

It seemed kind of stupid, but I politely said, "Well, I'll call back. Thanks for your help." I hung up. What help? Damned if I know, but politeness can sometimes be an irritating habit.

Wondering what to do next, I went out to the car and got out the Thomas Brothers map guide, the bible for anyone who drives in Los Angeles. I looked up Angela Sanchez's address and saw it was in East L.A. I decided to pay a visit.

First I swung by Little Tokyo and stopped at Fugetsu-Do. Fugetsu-Do is the oldest Japanese confectioner's shop in L.A. It's been in the same family for almost a century and they make what are positively the best *manju* (Japanese pastries) in town. I bought a nice assortment and watched as the clerk put them in a box and carefully wrapped the box with paper. Then she patiently tied a

red ribbon around the box and presented it to me. She did this on
every purchase, and if I had remembered to tell her this was a gift
she'd have used gift paper.

I stopped by the boutique and gave the box to Mrs. Kawashiri,
along with my thanks for setting up the meeting with Mrs. Okada.
Ongiri again.

Mrs. Kawashiri recognized the Fugetsu-Do paper immediately,
and after insisting that setting up the meeting was nothing, she
looked at the box and said, "Yumm! Can I look at them?"

"Of course. I hope you'll do more than look at them. With all
the pastries you've given me I owe you more than a few treats."

Mrs. Kawashiri opened the wrapping paper and took the lid
off the box. "My favorites! You have George's favorites, too."
George was Mr. Kawashiri. There is only a limited selection of
manju, so when you buy a large assortment it's hard not to have
people's favorites in it.

Happy that my small kindness was a success, I went back to
my car and drove to East L.A. and Angela Sanchez's address.

East L.A. is the modern Latino heartland of Los Angeles. Of
course, in the two-hundred-year history of the city, Los Angeles
has always been primarily a Latino city, but it's becoming even
more so because of a flood of recent immigration. Even the former
African-American bastion of Watts is now more than 50 percent
Latino. Despite the spread of Latinos in Los Angeles, East L.A. is
still special. It's where you find Latino families who have lived four
generations in the same neighborhood, and who have true roots
in both California and Mexico. Its blue-collar Mexican-American
population is an amalgam of two cultures, just like I am.

There are some aspects of Latino culture that mirror Japanese
culture. Both cultures share a respect for tradition, both are family oriented, and both make a virtue of hard work. Yet despite the
admirable traits of Latino culture, for a significant minority of Latinos in Los Angeles, something has gone wrong. The respect for tradition has been transformed into a bastardized collection of gang
signs, graffiti, and special gang clothing. The focus on family has
been turned into a travesty that encourages the creation of large
gangs or "crews" of taggers (organized graffiti vandals). The will-

ingness to engage in hard work has become a fountainhead for endless criminal activity, both great and small, and mostly dealing with drugs.

The result is hundreds, if not thousands, of Latino gangs in Los Angeles. Gangs are not just a Latino phenomena, of course, because there are also Anglo gangs, African-American gangs, and Asian gangs in Los Angeles. Crime seems to be an equal opportunity employer, although you rarely hear of a racially mixed gang. It's sad. It's also dangerous because gangs not only fight each other, they also prey on citizens of all races in the city.

I was mindful of this as I drove into the East L.A. neighborhood where Angela Sanchez lived. You'd have to be a fool not to be aware of it when you drive into neighborhoods strange to you in this city. In Angela's neighborhood the walls of almost every business were scarred with gang graffiti, along with many homes and apartment buildings. Groups of young men, some of them in gang-banger clothes, stood around on street corners engaging in mock fights and passing time. At minimarts banks of pay phones were arrayed outside, and better dressed youths stood waiting by the phones. Drug dealers waiting for their beepers to go off so they could buy and sell using public (and presumably untapped) phones.

A few stubborn residents maintained their houses with neat front lawns and graffiti-free walls. Even these bastions of middle-class normalcy exhibited the effects of the decline in the neighborhood because they invariably had bars on the windows and some even had fortified, wrought iron screen doors; the honest jailed in a desperate effort to keep out the predators that roamed free in the neighborhood.

Angela's address was an apartment building with four units. The street was strange because one side of the street had four- to six-unit apartments and the other side had single family residences. Angela's apartment seemed to be in pretty good shape, but the same couldn't be said for all the apartments on the block. Several had graffiti scrawled on them and the minimal vegetation in the front was dead. One of the apartments had an old, grease-covered engine block sitting in front of it on the curb, a monument to both someone's willingness to pollute the neighborhood while fixing a car parked at the curb and the city administration's indifference to cleaning up the streets.

On the other side of the street the homes were old, but many were well kept. On several fences facing the street I could see where graffiti had been painted over. An older Toyota truck was parked in one driveway and a new Chevrolet was in another. Up the block a garage sale seemed to be in progress. If you ignored the ubiquitous window bars, the side of the street with the homes could be a Beaver Cleaver neighborhood with a salsa beat.

One side of the street represented the old East L.A. of stable families and roots, the other side was the new East L.A. of transients with no stake in this neighborhood, city, or country. I felt proud and sad for the homeowners. Proud because they seemed willing to put up a fight for their neighborhood and sad because I thought the fight would be a losing one. Eventually the neighborhood would succumb to dirt and decay, and the homeowners would start losing their children to the gangs and the street.

I pulled up on the opposite side of the street from Angela's apartment and contemplated my next move. I've seen stakeouts a million times in movies and read about them even more, but the actual mechanics of a stakeout are something I've never given a lot of thought to.

I was an Asian sitting in a strange Nissan in a purely Latino section of town. I didn't have one of those special vans you see in spy movies and I couldn't afford to rent the proverbial apartment or house that always seems available, at least in fiction, across the street from the location under surveillance.

I stuck out like a sore thumb and the longer I sat there doing nothing the worse it became. I could pull up the block a distance so I wasn't sitting directly in front of Angela's apartment, but the people up the block might get alarmed or suspicious about someone sitting in front of their place for hours at a time.

There were also other practical problems to consider. If I left to get food it might be at exactly the time Angela chose to leave her apartment. Of course, I could go hungry, but sooner or later I'd have to go to the bathroom and the same problem would occur. And what if Angela wasn't in the apartment in the first place? This stakeout wasn't everything I figured it to be. Or more accurately, I hadn't figured things out at all when I drove over to her apartment.

At a loss for something more detective-like to do, I got out of the car and walked across the street. I went to the door of her apartment and knocked. Nothing. I knocked a second time and was starting to wonder what to do next when the door was suddenly opened. It gave me a little start, but not as big a start as the person I was confronting.

He was a man in his mid-thirties. He was shorter than me, which meant that he was really short, but what he lacked in height he made up for in muscle. The muscle was easy to see, because he wasn't wearing a shirt. It was a warm day, but not so hot that you'd expect to find people shirtless, and that surprised me a little. He was wearing scruffy jeans and equally scruffy cowboy boots with pointed toes. He was Latino, with a dark complexion baked a deep brown by exposure to the sun. His hair was greasy and curly, and worn in something that approached an old-fashioned flattop haircut. He did not look friendly.

"What do you want?" he said with a thick accent. A wave of sour beer breath rolled toward me. From the voice I thought it was the same man I talked to on the phone. On one bulging bicep he had a cross tattooed. On the other bicep he had "Jesus" tattooed. I didn't know if this was an epithet, a prayer, or simply a name.

"Is Angela Sanchez at home? I'd like to speak to her."

His eyes narrowed. "Who are you?"

"I met Angela a few nights ago and I'd like to talk to her." I wasn't anxious to give him my name.

His face darkened. "You think she's a *puta*? Is that why you came by? She likes you yellow types, but she comes home to a real man. You understand that?" He poked a stubby finger at me, and I thought he was going to step right into my face. I haven't been in a fistfight since grade school, but I thought I was going to be in one in about ten seconds. I stepped back and smiled with as friendly a smile as I could muster under the circumstances.

"Hey, there's no reason to get upset," I said. "I just wanted to talk to Angela. I really don't know her."

He seemed a bit befuddled. I don't know if the befuddlement was caused by the beer or by my reaction to his aggression. In any case, I decided it was a good time to make my escape with as much dignity as I could muster.

"Tell her I'll be back," I said, still smiling as I turned around to walk to my car.

"She's not here!" he shouted with a combination of anguish and anger that made me sort of believe him.

I walked to the car with my ears alert to the sound of the man running up behind me to attack me. Instead, I heard the door of the apartment slam shut. I started breathing again.

When I got to the car I felt as befuddled as Angela's boyfriend, husband, relative, or whatever he was. My first attempt at a stake-out was not a success, and I didn't know what to do next. It occurred to me that if Angela wasn't there, maybe her friend would go to her and I could follow him. Why he would do that instead of picking up the phone is something that didn't occur to me at the time. I was still shaken up by the reception I got at the apartment, and I just wasn't thinking clearly.

I decided to drive up the block and kill some time at the garage sale, keeping the apartment under surveillance.

The garage sale was being monitored by an older Latina and a young girl. The older woman might be in her late fifties or early sixties. She had on a brown cotton dress, and she was sitting on a folding chair. Glasses with a light brown plastic frame were perched on her nose. Next to her, sitting on the ground, was a small portable radio. The announcer on the radio was talking in Spanish, and he seemed to be pitching something hard. I caught the word "Mustang" and realized it must be a car commercial.

The young girl was around nine or ten. She was wearing a white cotton top with a pattern of tiny pink rosebuds. Her hair was in two braids with little pink ribbons at the end, holding the braids together. She had the ubiquitous jeans on, and they weren't the impossibly large-size jeans held up by a cinched tight belt like the gang-bangers wear. She was sitting on a little camp stool with a patient look that mirrored the older woman's. Grandmother and granddaughter, I guessed.

I stopped the car and got out. "Hi," I said to the older woman.

She seemed surprised to see me stop, and nodded to me gravely. She was uncertain about my intentions because she probably saw the incident at Angela Sanchez's apartment. What else was there to see on that street?

"I'd like to look over the stuff you have for sale," I said, waving at an array of junk spread out over two tables and also laying on her front lawn. I said that to let her know I wasn't a salesman. Another grave nod.

On the lawn was used clothing of various sorts. A lot of it was for infants or a very young girl, and I wondered if they were clothes that the young girl helping the woman had outgrown. On the tables were the jumbled collection of old appliances and odds and ends that you see at garage sales, but one item caught my eye, a Japanese samurai sword. Curious, I lifted it off the table and looked at it.

The scabbard was wrapped in fine black silk cords, wound tightly with the thin cords forming a pattern. The hilt of the sword was similarly wrapped, although a few of the cords were frayed. The sword guard was a simple black metal oval, with a grasshopper design in bas-relief on one side of the guard. I pulled the sword slightly out of the scabbard, and was surprised to see that the blade was engraved with a pattern. It looked like a temple sitting next to a river. The other samurai swords I've seen had a polished blade, and the only pattern on the blade was a wave or scalloped effect caused by the polishing. I'm not a sword expert, but the engraved blade made me think the sword might be a reproduction.

"This is a nice sword," I said. Another nod from the old woman. "Could you tell me where you got it?"

"My husband was in the army during World War Two," she said. "He picked it up right after the war when he was stationed in Japan. I think it's quite old, but now that my husband's gone I don't want to keep it around anymore." Her English had no accent, and I realized with a jolt that I've come to expect an accent from Latinos. It's the kind of racial stereotype I hate when people have similar expectations about Asians, and I was embarrassed and troubled by my own prejudice.

"How much are you asking for it?" I asked.

She looked at me shrewdly, sizing me up. "A hundred and fifty dollars," she answered.

I put the sword down. An unemployed person doesn't need an expensive samurai sword, even though I thought it would make a terrific prop for the L.A. Mystery Club mystery.

"I could go as low as a hundred," she added when I put the sword down.

"It's too expensive for me."

"I can't go any lower," she said with a note of finality.

"I'm sure that's a good price; it's just more than I can swing right now."

She looked disappointed, but didn't seem inclined to reduce the price any more.

I moved over to a pile of books at the end of the table. They were mostly children's books in both English and Spanish, including a couple of the Nancy Drew mystery books. I reached over to pick one up when I was suddenly shoved from behind.

The push propelled me into the table, jarring it from its position and spilling items to the ground. I spun around, and there was the man from Angela's apartment.

"How come you still here?" he said belligerently. He held up a large clasp knife and waved it at me.

In Luis Valdez's play *Zoot Suit*, the play starts with the narrator, dressed like a 1940's Chicano zoot-suiter, cutting his way onto the stage with a four-foot switchblade knife. It always gets a laugh because it plays off of an old stereotype about Latinos. The knife before me wasn't a switchblade, and it wasn't four feet long. But I can assure you it sure looked that big. And the guy holding it had evidently not been enlightened about the need to fight stereotypes. And I wasn't laughing.

Before I could say anything the old woman jumped up and started yelling in Spanish. The young girl ran for the house. My Spanish is almost nonexistent, but I got the impression that after she told the girl to run into the house she started berating the man with the knife.

He looked at her, then back at me. She must have been giving him a withering tongue-lashing, because he seemed to shrink back from the onslaught of her words. She was brave, defending a stranger from a knife-wielding drunk. When he looked at her again I reached on the table and picked up the samurai sword. I withdrew it from its scabbard, and when the man returned his attention to me, his eyes widened at the sight of me standing there with a real four-foot blade. He took a step back, which was a very good sign.

Emboldened by his retreat, the woman came around the table, still berating the man and shaking a finger at him. His ridiculous sense of machismo wouldn't let him make a retreat without having the last word, and he said something in Spanish to the woman, then said to me, "Don't come back."

Then he backed into the street, keeping a wary eye on the sword in my hand. He backed up almost all the way to his apartment, then turned around and retreated inside, slamming the door.

The woman and I looked at each other, and we started laughing. It wasn't laughter caused by amusement, at least on my part. It was laughter caused by relief.

"What's that guy's problem?" I asked.

"He's just bad. He drinks too much, and I think his girlfriend left him. Do you want my granddaughter to call the police?"

I considered that a moment, then I said, "No. Thanks to you and this," I lifted up the sword, "no harm was done. I'm glad that guy carries a knife instead of a gun. Are you going to be all right? I mean, he won't bother you because of this, will he?"

The woman snorted. It was a sound that eloquently expressed her contempt for the knife-waving neighbor.

I put the sword back into the scabbard, and I noted with interest that my hands weren't shaking. If asked, I'd have predicted an incident like this would have left me shaking like a leaf. Instead I seemed unusually lucid and alive.

I helped the woman put the dropped merchandise back on the table, keeping a wary eye on the apartment door. When I was done I decided that my first stakeout had certainly been eventful but not successful. But I did confirm that Angela wasn't at her apartment, which made me think she might be the woman I saw in Matsuda's room. Now the question was why she wasn't in her apartment. Was she scared or involved with Matsuda's murder or was it coincidental because she just wanted to dump her repulsive boyfriend/pimp/lover? I could add those questions to all the others I had. In fact, I even thought of another. I wondered if the police could be wrong about the murder weapon and if a large knife, like the one just waved under my nose, could have caused the wounds to Matsuda's body, instead of a sword.

While on the subject of swords, I looked at the samurai sword that had so recently come to my rescue.

"How much did you say you wanted for that sword?"

"A hundred dollars."

"Will you take a check?"

I play an ancient Japanese board game called *Go*. It uses round black and white stones to capture territory on a wooden board. Like chess, it requires a lot of study to get really good, and part of this study involves solving problems, usually printed in little books. Like chess problems, Go problems have a huge advantage over a real game. With a Go problem you always know there's a solution. They present the problem to you just so you can figure out the solution. In a regular game, however, you're presented with situations and you don't know if there's a solution for them or not. The problems presented by the L.A. Mystery Club were like chess or Go problems. You knew there was a solution and that all the pieces you needed to discover the solution were available to you. What I was facing now didn't have a guaranteed solution.

I felt frustrated. I was stuck. Well and truly stuck. Even asking myself the critical question ("What would Sam Spade do now?") didn't bring about a brainstorm.

Of course, the sensible thing would be to step back and let the cops do their thing, but by now you know I'm not all that sensible. My own resources had sputtered out, so I decided to ask the help of people who might apply more resources and intellectual firepower to the problem. I thought of Ezekiel Stein and Mary Maloney. I figured that the L.A. Mystery Club had sort of gotten me involved in this mess and maybe they had some ideas that could get me out.

Dale Furutani

I went to the office to check to make sure it wasn't ransacked again. Then I made a couple of phone calls to set up meetings with Ezekiel and Mary.

Ezekiel worked at the downtown DWP building. It was within walking distance of the office, but I knew that Ezekiel would validate my parking at the DWP parking lot, so like a typical Angeleno I drove.

The DWP building is a hulking monolith surrounded, appropriately enough, by a watery moat. The story of Los Angeles is really the story of water. Local supplies of water will only support 300,000 to 400,000 people, so for Los Angeles to exist it must import water from hundreds of miles away. William Mulholland built the L.A. Aqueduct around the turn of the century, and despite the fact that the city is built essentially on a coastal desert, L.A.'s growth has been fueled by cheap and plentiful water. Remember the movie *Chinatown*? That was a fictionalized account of what cheap water did for L.A.

In the last part of this century environmental and other interests have put a squeeze on L.A.'s profligate ways with water, but the city government and its water department still hasn't faced the reality of what that means yet. To me, the moat of water around the building is an apt symbol of the isolation from reality the city suffers from.

The Water Quality Division literally occupies the bowels of the building, stuck in the basement where there are no windows to let in the sunshine and light. I know I'm prone to finding symbols in things around me, but to me this was also apt. The people charged with preserving natural freshness and purity in the water were literally buried under the monolithic bureaucracy that reaches fourteen stories above them.

Ezekiel's office was tucked into a corner of the Water Quality Division. It was one of those semicubicles, with flimsy walls made of painted panels and glass. It was stuffed with papers, books, and blueprints. He waved me into the office and, without a word of greeting, waited for me to explain the situation.

It took me a while to explain everything that had happened. For most of my explanation he sat silently, playing with a pencil.

When I got to the part about Rita Newly and the two Asians in front of the office, however, he got animated.

"What did they look like?"

"Both Asians. One smaller than me, dressed in an expensive suit. The other one was twice my size, and dressed in a cheap suit. The big guy looked like a gorilla."

"Did they have all their fingers?" Ezekiel asked.

"That's a strange question." I thought for a moment. "You know, the big guy was missing the tip of a little finger on one of his hands. How did you know?"

"Yakuza," Ezekiel said. "Genuine Japanese Mafia, down to the missing the tip of his little finger. I bet if you peeled the shirts off them you'd find that one or both were tattooed."

"I don't think I want to know either one that intimately. You didn't let me finish, but I talked to someone from the *L.A. Times*, and he told me that Matsuda was associated somehow with Yakuza front companies."

"That's not a good sign. The Yakuza can be very, very dangerous."

"Don't they operate more or less openly in Japanese society?" I asked. "I mean, I was told they're involved in legitimate as well as illegal businesses."

"They do operate more or less openly. Some even have business cards identifying their gang and lapel pins with little logos. But that doesn't mean they can't be dangerous. That's how your friend, the big guy, lost his finger. When a Yakuza does something to offend his boss, his *oyabun*, he must make amends for it. Perhaps he botched a deal or failed on an assignment. But the way to traditionally make amends is to amputate a finger. It's called *yubitsume*."

"You know more Japanese than me," I said.

"Only crime words. I couldn't order a meal or ask where the bathroom is. But crime stuff I know."

"I suppose they call a particularly inept Yakuza stubby."

Ezekiel gave a half-smile, but then shook his head. "It's really not funny if you think about the discipline involved. They have to amputate their own finger. To show their sincerity to their boss, they'll stick their own finger on a chopping block and take a cleaver to it."

"Ugh."

"Ugh, exactly," Ezekiel answered. "If they'll do that to themselves, you can imagine what they will do to others. These are not people you want to mess around with."

"What are they doing in Los Angeles?"

"They're all over the Pacific. They're in Taiwan, Korea, Southeast Asia, and the Philippines. They're very active in Hawaii and they've started showing up here on the West Coast."

"What do they deal in?"

"Amphetamines, guns, prostitution . . . virtually anything they can make a buck at. Maybe it's amphetamines. That's the drug of choice in Japan and fairly easy to obtain in the U.S."

"The package I got for Rita Newly doesn't contain amphetamines. It contains this." I handed the sample warranty claims I had kept over to Ezekiel.

He studied them carefully and finally returned them to me shaking his head. "I'm a walking encyclopedia on crime, but the meaning of these claims has me stumped. It could be some kind of Yakuza scam, and it also could be that Rita is a victim of the Yakuza. Regardless, these invoices prove that story she told you about the pictures isn't true."

"Even I figured that out, Ezekiel. By the way, what did you mean about the tattoos and the Yakuza?"

"Yakuza also have a custom of tattooing themselves. Often they stop on the forearm, the neck and the calves of the legs, so that when they're in normal street clothes you can't see the tattoo. The rest of their body might be completely tattooed. It can cost thousands of dollars, and often they insist on having the tattooing done the traditional way, with ink and a bamboo needle. It can be quite painful."

"Sounds like these guys are into pain."

"I don't know if they're masochists," Ezekiel said. "They want to show discipline and how tough they are. If they're into pain at all, it's probably more likely they're into giving pain than receiving it."

"That's a jolly thought. You mean, they intend to be the giver, with me as the givee, if there's any pain involved?"

"Sounds like they had Rita Newly more in mind. Make sure it doesn't become you."

Ezekiel had no more words of real wisdom for me, so I left the DWP building and drove out to South Pasadena where Mary Maloney lives. I had never been to her house before, and the address she gave me was for a modest bungalow not too far from the Pasadena Freeway. It looked like one of those California Craftsman bungalows, with big wooden beams and beautifully manicured landscaping.

Mary greeted me at the door. She was a big woman, with a broad, ruddy face and brown hair. She's in her early forties, but she has one of those faces that probably looked the same at twenty. It isn't a beautiful face, but it has character and warmth, and it's the kind of face people trust immediately.

Mary was bundled up in a green knit dress and matching sweater when I got there, even though the air inside her bungalow was stagnant. I always thought that knit was not the most flattering choice for a woman of her size and, well, roundness. But she was happy with her wardrobe, so it was really none of my business.

The air in the bungalow was hot and stuffy. When I asked if the bungalow had air-conditioning, Mary seemed surprised that I wasn't comfortable. She walked to a wall and flicked on the air-conditioning, and a welcome coolness started cutting through the heat. On the wall next to the air-conditioning switch was a large canvas covered with paint squiggles. The whole living room was cluttered with paintings of all sizes, along with bronzes and small statuary. Incongruously, the room also had souvenir knickknacks. Things like little porcelain bells, decorative spoons, and little plates. Almost all of them had the names of cities all over the world painted or written on them (Tokyo, Rio, Milan, Toronto, Bombay, and, once again incongruously, Dayton, Ohio).

"That's an interesting painting," I remarked, pointing to the canvas next to the air-conditioning thermostat.

"Yes," Mary answered. "My father was interested in art. I can take it or leave it, myself."

"It sort of looks like a Jackson Pollock."

"It is."

"An original?"

"Yes. If you like art you might like to look at the pictures by the fireplace. There are a couple of Picassos, a Rembrandt sketch, and a Monet there."

"Originals?" I love art and my eyes were almost bulging out as I realized that art treasures were mixed in with all the cheap tourist souvenirs.

"Oh, yes. My father bought them years ago when they weren't that expensive."

"What does your father do?"

"He was a businessman," she said vaguely, "but he's dead now."

"Do you have an alarm system in this bungalow?"

"Yes, I do, but it's mostly for my protection. Thank you for being worried, but no thief will come in to steal artwork in this part of Pasadena. Thieves around here go for TVs and stereos, not Picassos and Rembrandts. That would require a professional art thief, and any real professional could defeat the typical home alarm system."

I wanted to talk art some more, but I could tell that I was making Mary uncomfortable. She had invited me into her home to help me with my problem, and I didn't want to repay her kindness by snooping. More important than art to me was the fact that Mary had a lively intelligence and was often the one who solved the Mystery Club's weekend mysteries. I hoped she could shed some light on mine.

We sat drinking tea in the small, musty living room while I told my story. When I was done she took the sample warranty claims from me and examined them carefully.

"What did Ezekiel say about these?" she asked.

"He admitted he was stumped, just like me. Do you have any idea what they're about?"

"No, but I know how to find out. You haven't tried the most obvious thing yet."

"Which is?"

"Call Mihara Electric and ask."

Mary picked up the phone and called, using the phone number printed on the invoices. Their U.S. headquarters is in Carson, California, a suburb of L.A. When the receptionist found out that she was calling about information on a warranty claim, she gave her another number and informed her that all warranty claims from dealers were paid through a central warranty office.

From the area code of the phone number given to her, Mary and I concluded that the warranty processing center was in the San Fernando Valley. Los Angeles is such a large conglomeration of people that it has multiple area codes.

"Get on the kitchen extension," Mary said as she dialed the warranty number. "You might find this interesting."

"Is that legal for me to eavesdrop?" I asked.

"Who's going to tell?" Mary said grinning. I figured she was right so I went into the kitchen and picked up the receiver. The kitchen was modest and neat and like her living room it was also filled with souvenir knickknacks. It also had an exquisite Degas painting of a ballerina hanging over the breakfast nook, an ancient looking Chinese scroll painting of an orchid, and a Remington bronze being used as a paperweight to hold down recipes torn from various magazines. I realized with a numbing impact that this little bungalow in South Pasadena must be filled with literally millions of dollars in art.

When Mary got through, she asked for some help on a Mihara Electric warranty claim, and she was connected to a claims processing supervisor.

"Can I help you?"

"Yes. My boss is out of town," Mary said in an amazingly girlish voice. "He's asked me to process a bunch of warranty claims for Mihara Electric products and I need some instructions on how to submit them to get payment."

"What's your dealer number?"

Mary read her the dealer number written on the claim form.

"Oh, that's a subcontracting dealer number. That means you're not one of our regular dealers."

"Is that common?"

"Sure. A lot of our warranty work is being done by subcontractors these days. Dealers are mostly sales agents, and a lot of them don't have comprehensive repair departments."

"Could you give me some information on what I'm supposed to do with these claims?"

"Well, are the claims stickered?"

"What do you mean?"

"Is there a small, white bar code sticker on the face of the claim?"

"Yes, all the claims have those kinds of stickers on them."

"Good. That means they've been reviewed and preapproved by the warranty department. All you have to do is mail them in, and we'll send you a check. Make sure that your business name and address is clearly noted on each invoice. We won't have your name and address in our warranty file, and if we don't have the address clearly indicated on the claim there might be some problem on getting your payment to you."

"The claims I have are for quite a lot," Mary said. "Do you think that will cause any problems?"

"How much are you talking about?"

"Over a hundred and twenty thousand dollars."

"That is a lot, but not too unusual. Usually that amount represents several month's worth of work."

"That's right," Mary said. "From the two claims I have in front of me, the dates cover two different months, so that appears to be the situation."

"I wish your boss submitted them as they were done, instead of accumulating so many at one time. But it really doesn't make much difference. We pay over two million dollars worth of claims per month. Just go ahead and send the claims in, and we'll get them processed. Don't forget to put your name and address on them. Like I said, as long as they've got their sticker on them, they're as good as gold."

"Okay," Mary said. "Thank you."

When I walked back into her living room, she waved the claim forms at me like a triumphant flag. "They're as valuable as cashier checks. Just about anybody can type a name and address onto the claim forms and collect a hundred and twenty thousand dollars, just like clockwork."

"A hundred and twenty-three thousand and something," I said.

"Don't be pedantic," Mary said. "Why do you think it's an odd number like that?"

"I don't know. Maybe she charges sales tax."

"Right."

"Okay. So maybe she doesn't charge sales tax. Maybe it's an odd number so it doesn't stick out on any reports," I said.

"What do you mean?"

"I mean odd numbers sort of blend in on any audit reports. If it came out to be an even number, like a hundred and twenty thousand or a hundred and twenty-five thousand, it would probably seem like an unusual coincidence to anybody looking over audit reports or computer listings of all the claims being paid during a particular month. Still, that seems like a large amount."

"Evidently not. You heard them say they pay over two million dollars in claims each month. Besides, all the claims have a dealer number that's evidently used by all subcontractors. It would be hard to trace that some new person has been receiving that amount of money."

"Why would someone want to do that?"

"What do you mean?"

"Get paid this way. Why not just give her cash?"

"I'm not sure, but I can think of a couple of reasons. One is that by doing it this way, Mihara Electric Company is actually footing the bill, either knowingly or unknowingly. Those little white stickers on the claim forms are approvals by the warranty department. Those could easily be stolen, or maybe Mihara is tied up with the Yakuza in some way.

"The second reason for receiving payment this way is that you'd be able to show some legal source for the money if you wanted to declare it on your income taxes. In fact, it also makes it a tax deduction for Mihara Electric, so Uncle Sam helps to partially foot the bill with this scheme."

"You mean someone who's going to get involved in something shady would be scrupulous on taxes?" I asked.

"You never know," Mary answered. "Remember, that's how they got Al Capone."

Mary gave me a lot to think about, both with the art stuffed in her bungalow and with the information about the warranty claims. I drove back to the office and opened the door to a persistently ringing phone. I thought it might be Michael Kosaka, because I gave him both my home and office numbers, and I dived for the phone.

I picked it up and recognized Mariko's voice.

"Ken?"

"Yes. You sound funny. Is something wrong?"

"Thank God you've returned. Please come to the boutique right away. Something bad has happened."

I left the office and half jogged to the boutique. When I got there a small crowd was gathered in front of it, peering through the window. I pushed my way through the crowd and got to the door where a uniformed policeman stopped me.

Past the policeman's shoulder I could see the boutique. It resembled the mess I had found the office in, but while the office was ransacked methodically, the clothes in the boutique were just scattered on the floor, with clothes racks tipped over in a haphazard fashion. Inside, another uniformed officer was talking to Mrs. Kawashiri, with Mariko hovering by.

"Mariko," I called. She saw me and walked over to the officer by the door.

"It's okay," she said to the policeman. "Please let him in. He's my boyfriend." The policeman shrugged and I stepped past him.

"What happened?"

"It was awful," Mariko said. Her frail body was shaking. I thought she was fearful, and I placed my arms around her shoulders.

"There's nothing to be scared of," I said. "I'm here now and so are the police."

Mariko's eyes flashed. "I'm not scared," she spat out. "I'm just so damn angry. If I had a baseball bat when that S.O.B. was in here, I'd have flattened him."

"What S.O.B.? What happened? What's going on?"

Mariko calmed herself down, taking a deep breath and gaining control of her anger. "About an hour ago a guy came into the boutique."

"Did you know him?"

"No," Mariko said. "He was a Caucasian, about six feet tall, light brown curly hair, muscular, with brown eyes. He wore a sports shirt and jeans. He seemed just like a regular guy. There was a customer in here when he walked in, and he waited until the customer left. When I asked if I could help him, he asked me if I knew Ken Tanaka. I thought he might be a friend of yours. He was leaning on the counter as nice as he could be." Mariko indicated the counter in front of the cash register. "Smiling, talking, and actually being quite charming. I told him that I did know you. He said that he was supposed to meet you here to pick up a package. He said he was in the neighborhood and decided to stop by early."

"Did he have a girl with him?"

"No. He was all by himself."

"Did you see somebody standing outside the shop? A blonde?"

"No. He just came in by himself, like he didn't have a care in the world. After I said I knew you, he said that he'd appreciate it if I gave him the package now, so he could save himself a trip coming back. There must have been something in the way I hesitated. That must have tipped him off that I either had it or I knew where it was. I must be a crummy actress!

"He started needling me about the package, saying it was okay for me to give it to him, that he and you were good friends, and that it would be a great favor to him so he wouldn't have to come back. I didn't know if he was a friend of yours or not, but I didn't think that he could have been a good friend, because in the time I've known you, you've never mentioned anybody with his name."

"What's his name?"

"Well, he called himself George Martin, but I doubt now that's his real name. Anyway, I started getting a little suspicious of the guy, so I told him that I didn't have any package here, and that he would have to come back and talk to you. That's when he started getting violent and abusive. He started raising his voice at me and pounding on the counter. He called me a Jap, a bitch, and a slut.

Then he started throwing things around." She waved her hand around the boutique. "He just started going berserk. He yanked clothes off the racks and threw them around, then he knocked the racks over."

"Then what happened?"

"By that time Mrs. Kawashiri came out from the back to see what the commotion was. When Mrs. Kawashiri saw what was going on, she ran in the back and got a knife she keeps back there to cut up bread for sandwiches. When she came back, she shouted at the guy to leave. You should have seen her yelling and waving around this little six-inch paring knife. I didn't know if I should be frightened for her or laughing. When the guy saw Mrs. Kawashiri with a knife, he hesitated. I don't know, Ken, but I thought maybe he might have had a gun tucked under his shirt or something. Anyway, he told me that I'd be sorry that I didn't give him the package when I had a chance, and he got out of here."

"Did you see which way he went? Or if he got into a car or anything?"

"No. We were all too shook up and upset. We called the police right away."

"Did he get the package?"

Mariko glared at me. "Of course not. It's still in the hatbox. Do you think I'm going to let a jerk like that intimidate me?"

I sighed. "I'll go apologize to Mrs. Kawashiri as soon as she's done with the police."

"Apologize for what?"

"I feel like I'm the one who's responsible for getting the shop wrecked."

"Aside from getting the clothes dirty," Mariko said, "he really didn't do any permanent damage. I'm just so angry with him. I'm going to buy a nice big aluminum baseball bat and keep it under the counter there, and if that guy ever walks into this shop again, I'm going to put a dent in that bat that matches the curvature of his pointed head."

The police finished and left the shop. I stayed to help Mariko and Mrs. Kawashiri clean up the mess. As we worked I brought both Mariko and Mrs. Kawashiri up to date on what I'd found out about the Yakuza and the value of the warranty claim forms.

Then, in Japanese fashion, I formally apologized to Mrs. Kawashiri for causing so much trouble. In an equally Japanese reaction, Mrs. Kawashiri absolutely insisted that no trouble had been caused, at least by me, and that I had no responsibility in the incident.

We both knew that I had caused trouble, and that I was in some manner responsible because it was my package that had triggered the problem. But despite the fact that both Mrs. Kawashiri and I are thoroughly Americanized in other parts of our lives, in our social interaction with other Japanese we play the complicated Japanese social ballet.

After making my apologies I said good-bye to Mariko and returned to the office. The phone was ringing when I got to the office, and I had a sinking feeling in my stomach that maybe it was Mariko calling again because something else had happened at the boutique. Instead, when I picked up the phone I was surprised to hear Rita Newly's voice on the line.

"Don't you have a service or answering machine?" she started, irritated.

"No, and before we continue this conversation, you're going to give me your phone number and your address so I can contact you when it's necessary."

After a moment's hesitation, she gave me a number and address in the San Fernando valley, which I wrote down on a slip of paper, along with her name.

"Now, I want my property," Rita said.

"I think a friend of yours has already tried to get the package."

"Meaning?"

"Meaning a Caucasian man calling himself George Martin just tried to tear apart the Kawashiri Boutique here in Little Tokyo, demanding your package."

Silence.

"I figure he must be a friend of yours. I told you the package was somewhere near my office and safe, so he probably hung around the office and followed me to the boutique. Unfortunately, that's not where the package is," I lied. "All he succeeded in doing was tearing up the shop and causing trouble."

"Damn!"

"Exactly."

"Look, Mr. Tanaka, I did have a friend of mine follow you, but he wasn't supposed to do anything. If he did something stupid, it was completely on his own. It's just that the package is very important to me, and I don't want to have to trust you without knowing where it might be." A pause. "Do you think five hundred dollars would cover whatever damage he might have done?"

"I'll check with the owner of the boutique and call you right back at the number you've given me." I figured I was being clever, checking that the phone number was valid.

"I'll be waiting."

I called the boutique, and Mrs. Kawashiri's warm and friendly voice came on the line.

"Mrs. Kawashiri, I just talked to the owner of the package, and she offered to pay you five hundred dollars for the damage caused."

"I don't want it."

"Isn't it enough?"

"I don't want the money. What I want to see is that guy in jail. He has no right to do this to my shop. He can't make things right by just paying for the damage he's done."

"I understand your feelings, Mrs. Kawashiri," I said. "But I really think you should take the money. It's being offered by the owner of the package, not the guy who was in your shop."

"Why?"

"Because she knows the guy. Besides, even if they do catch this guy and bring him to court, the chances of him really being seriously punished are almost nonexistent."

"But don't you think it's important for people to know they can't buy their way out of problems?" she said.

"Yes, I do. But sometimes what's important and what actually happens are two different things."

"Well, I don't like it," Mrs. Kawashiri said. "It's not right. It's just not right."

"Sometimes we can't always do what's right in this world. Look, how about this as a compromise?" I suggested. "Why don't you take the money to repair the damage done, but I'll tell them that the money doesn't absolve them of any criminal penalties which might be involved."

Mrs. Kawashiri considered for a moment, then said, "Okay. Let's try that. But I don't want any more than three hundred fifty dollars. That's what I think it will cost to clean the dresses that require it. I don't want any more."

"All right."

"Thank you for your help in this, Ken-san."

I hung up and called Rita Newly back and was almost surprised to hear her answering the phone.

"Mrs. Kawashiri only wants three hundred fifty dollars. That's all it will take to clean the dresses. She also wants you to know that this doesn't absolve your friend of any criminal charges."

"She doesn't want all the money?" Rita was incredulous.

"That's what I said."

"Fine. Now, how about my package?"

I checked my watch. "Well, I'm actually late for an appointment. I don't want to be petty, but I figure you can wait until after my appointment for me to call you and settle this package thing."

"Damn it, Mr. Tanaka . . ."

I gently put the receiver back on the hook. I was stalling because I knew I was going to turn the package over to the police. Besides, I know I said I didn't want to be petty, but I have to admit that there was a certain satisfaction in being petty, no matter what my better nature said.

On a whim, I called back to the boutique and asked Mariko if she wanted to have dinner. She told me that she was helping Mrs. Kawashiri take some of the dresses to the dry cleaners, and I immediately volunteered to help. Before leaving I took the two warranty claims out of my pocket and put them in the top drawer of the desk.

Mariko and I had dinner at the Ginza Gardens Coffee Shop. Then she asked me if I wanted to come to her place. "Maybe later," I told her. "I've been spending so much time on real mysteries that I'm falling behind on preparing for the L.A. Mystery Club's mystery. If I don't start working on it, there will be more than a few club members willing to kill me. How about I go back to the office for an hour or so, then I stop by your apartment?"

"Okay, but don't keep me waiting."

I returned to the office, and as I unlocked the door and walked in, a voice said, "You really should get a better lock for your front door."

I jumped from surprise and spun around. There, standing on either side of the door, were the two Asians who had scared Rita away. The small man gave me a grin, showing off some of the gold-capped teeth that festooned his mouth.

"We didn't want to wait in the hall," he added. "So we let ourselves in and made ourselves comfortable. The lock on your front door is ridiculously easy to open."

"Never mind the lock on my front door, what the hell are you two doing here?" I said.

"That's not a very warm greeting for two potential clients," the little man said.

"What do you mean?"

"Well, the sign on the door says you're a detective," the little man answered. "And we want you to find someone for us. Rita Newly."

"What do you want her for?"

"I think you know."

"I don't know."

"That's very good," the little man said.

"What are you talking about?"

"When you said you don't know, it had just the right ring of sincerity combined with anger at finding us in your office."

"Look, I'm not playing a game when I say I don't know what the hell's going with you two and Rita Newly."

The small man shrugged. He reached into his suit pocket and pulled out the two warranty forms. "These say different. It was careless to leave them in this office. Just because we searched it once, that doesn't mean we weren't going to search it again."

I calculated the odds of making it through the office doorway past the men. As if reading my mind, the larger of the two men stepped into the doorway, blocking it. He closed the door. The lousy latch made an ominous click, and despite what I had been told about how poor a lock it was, it sounded solid enough to me. Especially with a miniature gorilla standing in front of it.

"I wouldn't try it," the little man said. "My companion is very strong and quite good at the martial arts. More importantly, even if you were able to subdue him, you would then have to deal with me."

I shot a glance of surprise at the small man for this declaration of bravado. The man caught my glance and smiled once again. He reached into his other pocket and pulled out a small automatic pistol. The ugly blue-black barrel of the automatic pointed squarely at my midsection without a waver or a hint of hesitation.

"This makes me equal to just about anybody," the small man said. "Please don't do anything rash. This isn't one of the pieces of junk that Rita sold to my father in Japan. This is a pistol that I purchased right here in the United States, and I'm quite a good shot with it."

"What do you mean?"

"I mean I can kill you if I choose to or simply blow out your kneecaps and cripple you for life."

I felt I was in some kind of grotesque comedy. I explained myself. "I didn't ask your meaning to find out if you're a good shot. I was asking about what kind of junk Rita sold to your father."

"Surely, you know."

I sighed. I was scared and playing for time in the desperate hope that some bright idea would occur to me. "I really don't. Maybe I could help you if you'd explain to me what the hell's going on."

"Rita sold a shipment of pistols to my father in Japan. In Japan, firearms are strictly prohibited, and a good supply of guns is rather hard to come by. A four-hundred-dollar gun in the U.S. is worth five thousand dollars in Japan, to the right people. Rita arranged for a supply of pistols to be sent to Japan packed in a container of ball bearings. How she arranged that is her business, but what finally arrived in Japan turns out to be my business. The guns are junk, almost worthless. All of them are worn out, and some of them don't even work. They were probably destined to be sold as scrap. Instead, they were sold to us at quite a premium because of the difficulty of getting such merchandise into Japan." He held up the invoices. "Now we want to get the payment for that merchandise back. We also wanted to have a talk with Rita to explain to her that it's not nice to play such tricks on my father and to also ask her what she knows about the death of Matsuda-san."

"You weren't involved in that?"

"Of course not. Matsuda-san was a valuable member of our organization. That's why we want to talk to Rita about it."

"But not to me?" I didn't know if I should believe him about not being involved in Matsuda's killing. If he did confess to it, it was probably a bad sign for me because it meant that I probably wouldn't be around to tell anyone about it.

"You, too. Matsuda-san called us after he delivered the package to you. He was the one who gave us your name and address. He said you were simply a messenger boy and it made him suspicious that Rita didn't come by to pick up the package herself, or at least didn't send someone she worked with.

"Matsuda-san was no fool. He suggested that we should immediately contact Japan and have them check over the shipment of guns. He concluded that there might be something wrong with the shipment. The reason Rita hired someone to come by and pick up the payment was because she was afraid we might have discovered that the guns delivered were no good."

"Your English is very good," I said incongruously.

"Thank you," the small man said, pleased. "I went to USC. That's one of the advantages of having wealthy parents in Japan."

At my look of surprise, the small man grinned again. "It's hard to get into Japanese colleges, and private U.S. schools are so much more accommodating if you can pay the fees. It just takes wealth. Our wealth, of course, was attained through the Yakuza. In fact, you might say that I'm now following through with the family business, running the U.S. operations while my father continues to run things in Japan."

I looked at the bigger man. "And don't you ever say anything?"

The man looked back impassively, still blocking the door.

"No, he doesn't talk too much," the smaller man said. "But he can be very persuasive when he wants to be. As much fun as this conversation has been, I believe it's time that he does become very persuasive with you. Now, where can we find Rita and where can we find the rest of the warranty claims?"

With the smaller man holding the gun, I calculated the odds of getting out of the office were almost nil even if I was able to get past the stocky man in the doorway. I was actually surprised at how coolly rational my brain was working even as my body was making me feel sick with fear.

The small man shrugged. "I can see things are going to be difficult," he said with a sigh of what seemed like genuine regret. "I suppose you feel like the thing to do would be not to cooperate. I really don't think that's very smart, but some people have to learn the hard way."

He said something in Japanese to the stockier man, who strode forward, put his hand on my chest, and shoved me backward until I finally flopped into the chair behind the desk. The smaller man raised the gun to cover me as he said, "I wouldn't suggest you try anything."

The bigger man loosened my belt and slipped it out of the belt loops, then he used it to tie my hands behind my back, around the back of the chair. He pulled it tight, and the edges of the belt cut into the flesh of my wrists. When I was securely tied to the chair, the smaller man lowered his pistol.

"I wish you'd cooperate," the smaller man said reasonably. "I've been involved with several of these, and sooner or later people tell you what you want to know."

When the stocky man started the beating, he showed no pleasure in inflicting pain. In fact, he showed no emotion at all. It seemed like it was a rather boring job to him as his large callused fist came smashing down on my face. The force of the first blow was so sudden and jarring that I was more stunned than in pain. I wondered if my nose was broken, but I decided since the first blow had landed to the side of my face instead of straight on, that it was more likely that my cheekbone would be broken instead. Small comfort.

By the time the second blow was delivered, the anesthetic of fear and concussion had worn off and the pain started.

By the fourth blow, I started losing count. It looked as if the stocky man could continue pummeling me all evening with no apparent sign of fatigue. I remembered glancing over to the smaller man, to see him sitting at the edge of the desk looking very detached and patient. These men were professionals, I thought. They don't give a damn if I live or die, or if they beat me to death to get what they want to know. Another blow. But they probably won't beat me to death and they probably won't let me die. At least not yet. They'll just keep escalating to higher levels of pain until I finally tell them what they want to know.

Another blow. This one was so hard that I saw black spots in front of my eyes. There was a buzzing in my head. Through a red haze of pain I heard the smaller man talking in Japanese. I moved my head and pain shot through the left side of my face, causing me to groan. In my mouth I could taste blood.

I felt myself slipping into unconsciousness. I told myself I should give them Rita's address and stop all this. It was easy enough. The address was on a little slip of paper in my pocket and I'd just have to tell them about it. I actually wanted to speak up, but I couldn't because I was passing out. As I started slumping in the chair, I could hear Mrs. Kawashiri's voice from our earlier phone conversation ringing in my head. "It's not right, it's just not right . . ."

My face was being slapped, not brutally, but my cheeks were so bruised that it felt like I was being hit with a red-hot piece of iron. I was being revived from unconsciousness so the beating could start again.

When I was fully revived, the big Yakuza started hitting me again. I groaned from pain.

"Wait a minute," the small man said. He hopped off the desk and started looking through my pockets. I was almost grateful when he came across the note with Rita's address and phone number.

"Things are often simple," the small man said philosophically. "We were able to find the warranty forms in your desk, but I really should have searched you first. We might have been able to save ourselves a considerable amount of time and you a considerable amount of pain and grief. I just hope you've been getting some from Rita because I can't figure out why else you wouldn't tell us what we wanted to know."

He exchanged some words in Japanese to the stocky man. Then he said in English, "This is an old building without too many tenants, and it's nighttime. What I think we'll do is just leave you here with the doors closed, and I'm sure by tomorrow someone will find you. I don't think there will be anybody in the building to find you tonight."

He said a few more words to the stocky man, and they both walked out of the office, closing the door behind them.

I sagged in the chair. It took me several minutes to realize that I was crying. The hot tears ran down my face and dripped to my shirt front, which was splattered with my blood. I couldn't figure out if I was crying from the pain or from relief that they were gone and that I was still alive.

It seemed a long time before I heard pounding at the office front door. I heard a muffled, "Ken, are you in there?"

"Mariko," I croaked. My voice sounded oddly muffled, and the effort to shout her name left a strange ringing in my left ear. "Mariko," I tried again.

I could hear the outer office door rattling. They must have locked it behind them. I hoped that Mariko would be persistent enough to find a locksmith to get the door open.

There was some fumbling with the front door, and a few seconds later the door burst open. Mariko stood there, looking at me in shock and horror. "Oh, Ken," she said.

"Let me loose," I said. The words came out mumbled.

Mariko didn't understand exactly what I said, but she did understand what I wanted. She rushed across the room, and I could feel her fingers tugging at the knots in the belt that bound my hands. After a few seconds she stood up, opened the desk drawer, and rummaged through the desk until she found a pair of scissors. She used the scissors to gnaw at the belt until she finally cut through it and released my hands.

"I got worried when you didn't show up," she said. "I'll get an ambulance." She reached for the phone.

"No, not yet," I said. This time she was able to understand me. She looked confused and indecisive, unsure if she should follow my instructions or go ahead with her instincts.

I tried to think, trying my best to remember the phone number Rita had given me. "Got to call Rita Newly," I mumbled. "Those guys are going there next."

I put the phone up to my ear and winced as the receiver made contact with my bruised skin. I dialed, trying to think of alternative combinations just in case I didn't have the number right. I was lucky.

Rita Newly answered the phone on the first ring. "Hello?"

"They're coming to get you," I mumbled. "The two guys from the Yakuza."

"Who is this?"

"Tanaka."

"You sound funny."

"I got beat up."

There was a pause. "Are they going to the address that I gave you earlier today?"

"Yes."

Another pause. "Get out," I said.

"That's not my real address," she said. "It's just an address I made up this morning. I didn't want you to know where I live. The phone number I gave you is for a cellular phone."

"Damn it. If I had known that, I could have given them that damn address and saved myself a beating."

"I'm sorry, Mr. Tanaka. But I still want my property," she added.

"You're relentless, aren't you?"

"It is my property, Mr. Tanaka."

"Okay. I'll give you your damn package tomorrow at four o'-clock." I said the first place that popped into my head. "The sculpture garden at UCLA. Meet me there at four o'clock, by the statue of a kneeling woman."

I wanted to slam the phone down onto the cradle, but I was too weak. Instead I just handed it over to Mariko who hung it up.

"Come on," she said. "Now I'm going to call an ambulance."

"No," I said.

"Are you crazy? If you saw how you looked you wouldn't be trying to play Mr. Tough Guy with me."

"I didn't say I wasn't going to go see a doctor. Why don't you drive me down to the emergency room? I just don't want an ambulance. Then I want you to hunt down your cousin Michael's home phone number for me. I want to talk to him and get some things settled tonight. By the way, how did you get in?" Although it hurt, my mouth seemed to be working better now.

"I used a credit card to slip the lock on the door. I saw it in a TV movie once."

I really do have to get a better lock for the front door, I thought.

The Franklin Murphy sculpture garden at UCLA is an oasis in the bustling hub of Westwood, a suburb of Los Angeles. It has winding paths, cool trees, and a surprising collection of modern and traditional sculpture, including a Rodin torso, a Matisse collection of bronze plaques, and some pieces that are decidedly more modern, including a sculpture that is a puzzling collection of painted blue tubes welded together.

On Sunday mornings Mariko and I would sometimes go to the sculpture garden to have a picnic. Nestled in the curves of the winding paths of the garden are concrete seating areas that look very much like military bunkers. They're round circles of cement approximately twenty feet across and four feet high. The center of the circle is empty and a wooden bench hugs the inside curve of the concrete so people can sit and rest. In many of these little enclaves, smaller pieces of sculpture reside, poised on a pedestal in the center of the circle. Entrance into the center of the circle is through a narrow cut in the concrete only a few feet across, and once into the center of the circle, peace and a kind of solitude can be found.

Down a path in the garden, heading toward one of these concrete bunkers, walked Rita Newly and her companion. She wore a pale, lavender summer dress with Porsche sunglasses propped up on her forehead. Under her arm she carried a lavender leather purse to match the color of her dress. The man was tall and muscular. He was wearing gray slacks and a short-sleeve white knit shirt that showed his muscular arms to good advantage. Rita and the man made a smashing couple.

On the grass by Bunche Hall is a bronze statue of a nude woman crouching down and looking over her shoulder. The flesh of the woman is done in sweeping curves, and the expression on her broad, almost Asian face is enigmatic. Rita and her companion cut across the lawn to stand by the statue. She checked her tiny silver and diamond wristwatch. "It's four o'clock," she said.

"I wish you'd never gotten involved with that damn Jap," her companion said.

"Which one?" she asked. "Matsuda or Tanaka?"

"Both. This is turning into a royal pain in the ass."

She looked over at her companion and examined him as if she was looking at a new and particularly puzzling type of insect life. He was certainly handsome enough, with light brown curly hair, brown eyes, and the kind of tan that can only be obtained by people who are serious about sitting around in the sun until their skin baked to a crispness that is perceived as being healthy, even though it is more often a precursor of skin cancer.

"You're the one who was scared to pick up the package," she said. "You were afraid they might have found out that the guns we sent were junk."

"I wasn't afraid," he said defensively. "I just thought it would be a better idea if we got someone else to pick up the package, just in case."

"You weren't willing to go and pick up the package from Matsuda, so I had to make arrangements to have it picked up. I sure as hell wasn't going to go up there by myself. I don't need any second-guessing from you about what I did or how I did it, especially when you tried to pull some strong-arm stuff in that boutique instead of waiting like I told you."

Rita saw a flash of anger in her companion's eyes, and for a minute she thought she had revealed too much of her thoughts. "I'm not trying to blame you, honey," she said hastily. "I just want you to know it isn't my fault, either. I'm upset that we have to wait so long to get our money, too." Rita saw the anger subside in his eyes at the sweet reasonableness of her apology.

She reached over and patted him on the cheek. "We're so close to getting the money that we really shouldn't be fighting."

"Damn it, where the hell is that Jap," the man said.

"We don't like being called Japs," I said as I stepped out of the concrete seating area adjacent to the statue. "This is hardly a social occasion, but you can try saying Japanese until we're at least done with our business."

I was dressed in a sports shirt and blue jeans. My face was puffy with large black and red spots, and I had a gauze bandage taped to my cheek.

Rita saw the condition of my face and opened her mouth like she was about to comment, but she closed it again. Instead, she said, "Do you have the package?"

"Yes, I do. But I thought it might be better for us if we conduct our business inside this seating area where we can have some privacy."

She nodded and walked toward the concrete circle with her companion trailing behind. When she got inside the circle, I pointed to a section of bench with a mock gesture of gallantry. "Please sit down," I said. "There's no reason we have to be uncomfortable."

Rita sat next to me. She angled her legs so her knee was touching mine. Her companion sat down next to her, poised on the edge of the seat, acting fidgety and nervous.

"I suppose this is George Martin?"

"His real name is George. I don't think we have to go into last names," she said.

"And is your name Rita Newly?"

She smiled. "Well, the Rita part is right, and I don't think we have to go into real last names for me, either."

I nodded. She leaned her leg into mine. I could feel the soft warmth of her thigh and the gentle, almost caressing, pressure. Despite her beauty, I no longer found it affecting me. Instead, I could observe her little techniques and tricks with sort of a cool, clinical detachment. "I believe you owe me three hundred and fifty dollars for the damage your friend George did to the Kawashiri boutique."

"Are they sure they don't want the full five hundred?" Rita said.

"Three hundred and fifty is all she wants."

"All right," she said. She opened her purse and took a small stack of bills out. I extended my hand as she counted out the three hundred and fifty.

"All right," I said. "Now I think we're even. Your friend George should know that Mrs. Kawashiri still intends to press criminal charges if the chance comes up. Here's your package." I reached under the bench and pulled out the package.

Rita took it out of my hands immediately. "It's been opened," she said.

"That's right," I answered. "And two of the warranty claims are missing."

"What the hell's going on?" George started.

"Take it easy," I said. "That's how I got this." I pointed to my face. "I lost two warranty claims to your friends in the Yakuza. They told me what this is all about and explained to me that they were not exactly happy that the load of guns you shipped them are defective. In fact, if they catch up with you, I think they'll do considerably more to you than they've done to me. Believe me, what they did to me was more than enough."

"That's a very accurate observation, Mr. Tanaka." The small Yakuza walked into the circle of concrete followed by his hulking companion. Rita's friend, George, looked around wildly for an avenue of escape.

The concrete bunker formed a cul-de-sac that neatly trapped us with the two Yakuza standing at the only entrance. George started to stand up to climb over the surrounding concrete to get away. The small man produced his gun. "Don't do that. It would be very messy if I have to scatter your guts over this fine public institution." He looked at me with a twinkle in his eye. "Although, being from USC I guess I really shouldn't care how messy I get the UCLA campus." UCLA and USC are crosstown college rivals in Los Angeles.

"Look," George said. "I really don't know what this is all about. I'm just Rita's boyfriend. I just came along because she asked me to."

"Oh, shut up, George." Rita's voice carried the sting of a whip to it, and George flinched as if he had actually been struck by that whip.

"How are you, Toshi," she said with much more sugar in her voice.

The small man smiled. "Hello, Rita. You really shouldn't have tried to play these kinds of games with us."

"You two know each other?" I said.

"Oh, yes," the small man said. "Rita used to work for us in Japan. She was one of our best singers, dancers, and all-around entertainers." He gave her a huge grin. "And when she was done with her contract, she told us that she could do business with us to help us get guns into Japan. We paid her a large sum of money, but they turned out to be junk. Where did you get so many junk guns, Rita?"

"We bought them from local police departments," Rita said. "George has a federal gun license. It only takes a few hundred dollars to get one. He can use that license to buy surplus guns from police departments."

"You bought the junk guns from police departments?" Toshi seemed amused.

"L.A. doesn't sell the guns it seizes, but smaller police departments all over the state do."

"Interesting, but they're all junk. They're no good to us."

"But smuggling them in with the ball bearings did work," Rita pointed out. "George still works for the ball bearing company. He could arrange another shipment. He could use his gun license to buy good guns this time."

"That's a very interesting offer," the small Yakuza said. "but I'm afraid it's a Japanese trait to have a very long and very persistent memory. If I was a western businessman, I suppose I might overlook what we could term some irregularities with this current shipment and we could make some arrangement for conducting business together in the future." Another big smile. "With, of course, some preliminary quality control inspections before the shipment is sent off to Japan. But, you see, my father is not a western businessman and in some respects neither am I. I don't think we care to do business with you in the future. In fact, we don't want to do business with you ever."

"The claim forms are here," Rita said, showing him the package. "There's really no harm done. You could take them back, and maybe you can let me go."

"Well, that's certainly something worth considering. Especially for you, Rita. But my father would get very unpleasant even to his own son if he found out that I was playing games, too. Besides, what about poor old Matsuda-san? I didn't like him very much, but he was extremely useful to my father and the various family enterprises we have."

"We had nothing to do with Matsuda," George said hastily.

"That's right," Rita confirmed. "In fact, we didn't even go over there to pick up our payment. This is the guy who went over to pick up the payment."

I noted with amusement that Rita's thigh was no longer touching mine. I half expected her to leap up pointing an accusing finger at me.

"Good try," the small man said. "But Matsuda phoned us after he delivered the package, so we know this guy wasn't involved with his murder. We thought you might have killed him after this guy picked up the package."

"So you guys didn't kill Matsuda?" Rita asked.

"Of course not. Why would we want to do that? Like I said, he was valuable to us. I've been sort of working on the theory that you did it, although I have to admit that I can't imagine you using those delicate white hands to hack up his body with a sword."

"We didn't do it. You have to believe us," George said.

"Oh, I believe you," the small man said. "What my father is angry about is the load of defective guns you sent to us. It made him lose a great deal of face, especially since it was done by a woman. You know how much face is worth in the Orient."

The late afternoon sun caught the gold on his teeth as he smiled again. "It might even be a life and death matter," he said. "Now, come on. We want to drive you out to some place so we can talk about this with a little bit more privacy. Maybe you can convince me that you didn't kill Matsuda. Hell, maybe you can even convince me that we should still do business on guns together. Too bad for you if you can't." He smiled and motioned with his gun. "Come on. We have a car waiting in the parking lot, and we're all going to walk there nicely without any heroics or any attempts to escape.

George and Rita reluctantly got to their feet.

"You, too," the Yakuza said to me. I stood up slowly. "Now, you three walk in front of us, and my companion and I will be right behind you. Like I said, don't try anything funny."

Rita, George, and I moved as a group across the entrapping circle of the seating area. At the entrance, we brushed past the two Yakuza and walked out onto the grass. The two Yakuza were right behind us.

As the two gangsters cleared the concrete of the seating area, a voice shouted, "Freeze! Police!"

I turned around in time to see a look of surprise cross the face of the small Yakuza.

"Put your hands in the air."

The small Yakuza shrugged and said, *"Shigata ga nai,"* Japanese for "what the hell," or "it can't be helped." He took his hand out of his pocket and slowly raised both hands in the air, saying something in Japanese to his companion, who also raised his hands.

Three uniformed LAPD officers, a lieutenant, and Detective Hansen stood from where they had been crouching near the entrance to the concrete seating area. One of the LAPD officers was a woman.

"Thank you, officers," Rita Newly began.

"That means you, ma'am. Put your hands up, too."

Looking indignant, Rita Newly raised her hands. In one hand she clutched her purse. In the other was the envelope with the phony warranty claims. George started putting his hands in the air, but suddenly bolted past me in a stupid effort to escape. Before the police officers could react, I stuck out my foot and tripped him.

He took a beautiful skidding dive right onto the concrete walkway. I gave it about an 8.7, with extra points for landing chin-first on the concrete. In a second the officer had pounced on him and had him handcuffed.

I know it wasn't much but it actually felt good to give a little physical punishment back after suffering it myself.

"He's got a gun in his pocket," I said, pointing to the Yakuza. The officers immediately handcuffed and started patting down the Yakuza and the still-prone George. Rita got handcuffed and the policewoman patted her down, too, to a storm of invective. Rita had a small, rather dainty chrome automatic with a pearl handle in her purse. An eye for fashion, even in killing instruments.

After Rita, George, and the Yakuza were removed, I unbuttoned my shirt and one of the officers started gingerly removing the tape holding the transmitting device and microphone to my chest.

"Did you get everything? Including what they said before they came into the seating area?" I asked Lieutenant Jarvis Johnson.

"Every golden word," Johnson answered. "Although I wish somebody would have confessed to Matsuda's murder, instead of all of them standing around denying it."

I snorted in disgust. "There should still be a tasty assortment of charges that you can nail them with."

"Yeah, but I think most of them are federal raps," Lieutenant Johnson said.

"I'll try to remember that the next time I play human microphone. You know, make sure they only cover state and local offenses."

"All right," Johnson said. "I don't mean to sound ungrateful. It just would have been nice to wrap up Matsuda's murder along with everything else. They could all be lying, of course, but it would have just been nice."

I nodded as I handed over the transmitting device and microphone. That I could agree with.

Michael Kosaka had arranged for me to meet with Lieutenant Johnson that morning to explain the situation and turn over the package. Michael had said that it might be better dealing with Lieutenant Johnson, who happens to be African-American. Michael said cryptically that Detective Hansen had some past problems dealing with minorities, but he wouldn't elaborate. I looked over at Hansen, who had stood like a mute during the entire bust. He was looking at me with a look of pure hate. I realized I had made an enemy, one I might be sorry about if I kept poking around in police matters.

20

Y ou're a hero."

"No, I'm not."

"Oh, come on," Mariko cajoled. "None of this phony modesty. You helped the police round up two gunrunners and the two Yakuza who beat you up. I'm sure when they start checking into them, they'll find other things that they can nail them for. I just think it's great, and I'm really proud of you."

"Well, maybe it wasn't too bad," I said, giving her what I thought was a suitably modest smile. She threw her arms around my neck and kissed me. A big, wet kiss. "Ouch!" I said. "Take it easy. This face of mine still feels like a piece of raw hamburger. Even your kisses can't change that."

We were both sitting on my couch. After making the necessary statements to the police I drove home after my encounter with Rita, her lover, and the two Yakuza at UCLA. Mariko was waiting for me, a nervous wreck. She insisted that I go through the encounter in detail, something I was not particularly adverse to doing.

"Oh, I almost forgot the best part," I said.

"What's that?"

I reached into my pants pocket and pulled out a wad of bills. "Here's the three hundred and fifty for Mrs. Kawashiri. I figure I came out short a couple of hundred, but Mrs. Kawashiri should get what's due her. Rita said she'd pay me five hundred dollars to pick up the package and deliver it, and I only got three hundred. Well, I picked up the package and delivered it. I told her as long as she wasn't involving me with something that was illegal, I'd keep her confidentiality, and that's exactly what I did. As soon as I found out what the scam was, I didn't have second thoughts about calling the cops in. When the two Yakuza guys showed up it was lucky I did. I didn't get the full five hundred dollars, but I figure the initial three hundred dollars she gave me is mine. Not bad for just a few days' work."

"A few days' work and getting your face rearranged."

"Oh, yeah. That, too. You know, I just realized I owe your cousin Michael two hundred fifty dollars. That means I cleared a whopping fifty bucks. In fact, when you deduct my medical expenses, I'm going to end up with a net loss on my first foray into big-time detective work."

"It wasn't worth it, Ken, and it's not a matter of money. Even if you made a ton of money, it's just not worth it."

I sighed. "I know. Every time I move and feel the pain, I know that. But it still makes me happy to have the money for Mrs. Kawashiri. Why don't you give it to her tomorrow?"

"All right. I'm sure she'll be surprised to see it. Well, aside from the minor point of getting your face pushed in and almost killed, this entire case has been a triumph for my ace detective."

"Not exactly."

"What do you mean?"

"I still can't figure out who killed Matsuda. They all denied it."

"And they're all liars."

"Well, that's true," I said. "Rita's boyfriend, George, sure had a temper violent enough to have him hack up Matsuda, although he hardly looks like the type to carry a sword around tucked away for just such occasions."

"What about the Yakuza?"

"Well, the sword is a Japanese weapon, and those guys can get really nasty. But you know, despite the beating they gave me, I got the feeling that they were very professional in the way they went about doing things. That if they killed Matsuda they'd just simply kill him and not hack up the bits after he was dead."

Mariko gave a little shudder. "Maybe they hacked him up before he was dead."

"Well, that's a possibility. I suppose if they wanted to know something from him or if they were really bent on revenge, they'd do something like that. You know, it's a pet theory of mine that violent crimes like this are done by psychopaths or people with a long-standing grudge. It's still a puzzle to me."

"Why don't you let the cops handle it? You've already handed them enough on a silver platter."

"You're probably right, but it still bugs me. Look, I know you want to talk some more about this, but I'm really beat." I laughed. "Literally beat! Do you mind very much if we went to bed right now?"

I fell asleep with Mariko curled up in my arms. During the night I woke with a cry, my heart pounding and my breath coming in gasps. I had dreamed that I was still tied to the chair in the office with the edge of my belt cutting into the flesh of my wrist, while a mechanical Yakuza was beating me. The big Yakuza was now a shiny machine with flailing arms that swung toward me in wide arcs as the machine twisted from side to side. The arms didn't actually hit me, but with each swing they came closer and closer to my face. Since the Yakuza was a machine, there was no one to appeal to and no way to shut it off. The clenched fist at the end of the swinging arms came closer and closer to my face, and right before they hit I woke up.

"It's all right," Mariko said. Now her arms were holding me, pressing me against her naked bosom. My face was so battered that Mariko pressing me to her breast actually caused me pain and I had to push myself away slightly to take the pressure off my cheek. Despite the tenderness of my face, I didn't want to distance myself too much from her and her smooth skin. She felt warm and strong in the darkness around me.

"I had a nightmare that I was still in the office being beaten."

"I heard you crying out," she said. "But you're safe with me now. They've been put away. You put them away. It's going to be all right." She held me closer and this time I didn't push myself away, even though it was slightly uncomfortable to my bruised skin.

When my breathing turned from short gasps to a regular rhythm of inhale and exhale, she started stroking my hair, kissing me gently.

"I guess I'm not as tough as I think I am," I said, a little embarrassed.

"Nobody is. But you sound like that's something to be ashamed of. It's okay to be gentle, scared and lonely and in need of a friend sometimes. I know I am, and I know one of the things I love about you is that I always feel like you'll be there when I need a friend."

I closed my eyes, and after a few minutes I calmed down enough to slip back into sleep.

It was a night for dreaming. Or maybe nightmares. Most Asian cultures put a great store in dreams, and there's some residual part of my psyche that also places great faith in dreams.

When I fell asleep again I dreamed I was back in Hawaii at *O-bon* time. *O-bon* is the Japanese Buddhist festival of the dead. Like I said, Little Tokyo in Los Angeles sort of celebrates it during its Nisei Week, and maybe that's what set me dreaming about it, but in Hawaii we really celebrate it.

During soft August nights the Japanese believe spirits of the dead return. In the darkness the spirits float close to the ground, like a mist, and they move in and out of our lives as if they were still alive. In Hawaii everyone celebrates *O-bon,* whether they're Buddhist or not. During this time Buddhist entice the dead near with offerings of large, round *mochi* (pounded cakes of sweetened rice) and bright *mikans* (the tangerine-orange).

When I was a kid growing up in Hilo after World War II the local Buddhist church would set up booths for an *O-bon* carnival. The carnival was a fund-raiser for various church activities. Even though I was a Methodist I'd go to the Buddhist carnival to have fun. Everyone did.

One booth at the carnival would sell cones of shaved ice crystals covered with flavored syrup, a treat popular in Hawaii. For twenty-five cents you could get any combination of flavors you wanted. My particular favorite was half lime and half grape, but

I tried all the permutations of flavor that can be made from six different syrups. A particularly strange combination was called the rainbow, which consisted of all six flavors: lime, grape, strawberry, rootbeer, orange, and a vile yellow liquid they called melon. Melon is a flavor favored by Japanese, but it was too strange and musty tasting for me.

At another booth you could get toasted mochi. These were miniature versions of the pounded rice cakes, which were set out as offerings to the dead. These *ko-mochi,* or baby mochi, were toasted over an open gas jet. They'd turn puffy and expand, bubbling up into weird shapes and forming a toasty, golden shell over the warm, sticky insides.

When you bought a ko-mochi they'd toast it right in front of you, then they'd give it to you on a small paper plate with a little mound of mixed sugar and cinnamon. You'd dip the hot mochi into the sugar and cinnamon mixture and try to eat it quickly without burning your mouth, before it cooled down and lost flavor.

At night during the carnival, in the open field next to the Buddhist church, they'd build a large bonfire. They'd set up loudspeakers at the edge of the field and play scratchy records of bright Japanese folk music, all syncopated and full of the sounds of strange instruments you don't find in Western music. To the sound of this music the people would gather and dance *Odori* dances around the fire, wearing Japanese *yukatas,* or summer kimonos, and Japanese wooden slippers, called *getas.* The wooden getas would make a syncopated sound as they slapped the Hawaiian earth.

In the Hawaiian sky a big round moon will hang, flanked by countless hard, bright stars. These are the same stars that guided the ancient Polynesians to the islands. They're the stars that Captain James Cook navigated by when he "discovered" the islands. They're the same stars used to provide reference points when the souls of the dead descend from heaven to earth to join in the festivities of the humans still on earth.

The dancing people will move their hands and twist their bodies in stylized motions that were originally developed by Japanese peasants, who used the motions of the dance to mimic the motions of their everyday lives, illustrating things like planting rice or harvesting barley or pulling on the lines of a large fish net. The fire crackles and the outline of the dancers make a hypnotic wave against the orange and red flames. Sparks fly up, ascending to heaven.

In my dream I could hear the music and see the dancers rhythmically circling the bonfire, doing a dance where they dipped low and then put their arms up toward the sky. As they circled I could see one dancer who looked peculiar to me. It took a second, but I realized that the dancer was missing an arm.

As the circle of dancers made their way around the fire I could gradually see that the dancer with the missing arm was Matsuda. His face wasn't horribly sliced like it was in the pictures I had seen. In fact, it was quite intact and passive and held no emotions. The dancing light from the bonfire played across it, illuminating everything but the eyes, which remained shrouded in a velvet blackness. The dancers around the ghostly figure of Matsuda were laughing and enjoying themselves, but the one-armed apparition showed no human feelings as it went through the mechanical motions of the dance.

The circle of dancers continued to move around the bonfire, and eventually Matsuda's figure was on the opposite side of the circle, where it was obscured by the leaping flames of the bonfire. Matsuda's dancing figure looked like a lost soul, caught in the flames of hell.

Suddenly in my dream someone was standing next to me, and I was relieved to turn and see it was Mrs. Kawashiri. Her usually sunny face looked quite serious, and she waved a finger at me like she was lecturing a child. "It's not right, it's just not right," she said.

T he next morning I woke to an empty bed. On Mariko's pillow was a note that I picked up and read:

Ken-san,

Had to go to work. You were sleeping so soundly, I didn't have the heart to wake you. I made you breakfast. (How domestic! Fair warning—I have my sights set on you, and you know how persistent Japanese girls can be!)

Your breakfast is in the oven staying warm. I'll talk to you after work—Pick me up!—We'll celebrate you cracking the case. (We'll go someplace—my treat!).

Love,
M

I got up and found a breakfast of scrambled eggs, toast, and sausage waiting for me in the oven of my tiny stove. Sitting at my table, spreading strawberry jam on my toast, I reflected that I was unemployed, over forty, and beaten up, but that I could be doing a lot worse in life.

I went over to the doughnut shop and bought a copy of the *Times.* There, buried in the Metro section, was a small story about the police arrests of Rita Newly and the two Yakuza. The article referred to the Yakuza and Rita as suspects in the murder of a Japanese businessman in Little Tokyo, as well as other crimes. The reference to the murder of Matsuda left a nagging thought in my mind that I turned over and over.

I'm not a good cook, but I do have a couple of dishes I like to make. On occasion I've made a dish and found that my meager kitchen was missing a spice or herb called for in the recipe. I've gone ahead and made the dish, but it didn't taste quite right. Matsuda's murder didn't taste quite right.

The Yakuza were the prime candidates for the murderers. Evan Okada told me they liked to use swords, and Ezekiel told me the Yakuza could be very nasty characters. More importantly, I wouldn't believe anything the Yakuza said so their denial about their involvement in Matsuda's murder was worthless to me. Still, Matsuda was their man, and although he could have done something that would make them want to eliminate him, it still didn't taste right.

Rita's boyfriend George had a temper and Rita was as cold as they come, but although I could see either of them plugging someone with Rita's little chrome pistol, I couldn't see them hacking away at someone when pulling a trigger would do. That didn't taste right, either.

Angela Sanchez was an enigma. I still didn't know for sure if she was the woman I saw in Matsuda's room. Her boyfriend (or whatever he was) was a nasty character in his own right, but I found it hard to believe the police could mistake wounds caused by a large knife with wounds caused by a sword. That didn't taste quite right, either.

Feeling restless, I put on some shoes and decided to take a walk around Silver Lake. Silver Lake is one of the oldest reservoirs in Los Angeles and one of the few that remain open despite efforts by the Department of Water and Power to cover it. It covers seventy acres and there's another small open reservoir called Ivanhoe directly adjacent to it that's another ten acres. Los Angeles has about a tenth the open space that urban planners says is desirable, and in a city with so little open space, finding such a large expanse of open blue water right in the center of the city is both a treat and a solace. That's the reason local residents and environmentalists fought hard to prevent the DWP from covering it.

If you live in Oregon or Canada or someplace like that, the things that city dwellers try to save must seem pathetic. When faced with the grandeur of the Columbia River Gorge, for instance, Silver Lake seems pretty puny. Despite its name, it's not even a real lake. It's a man-made reservoir with concrete sides. Yet most people have a need to cling to some kind of nature, and if carelessness and the march of civilization has wiped out the grand examples of nature around you, then you fight to preserve what is left. I grew up in Hawaii, where I was never too far from the ocean. Around me was lush tropic vegetation with flowering ginger, hibiscus, and spreading banyan trees. In Los Angeles the closest thing I can come to that is a hibiscus bush that grows in front of my apartment. You take what you can get.

My apartment is about a ten-minute walk from the water. Although the reservoirs are bounded by curving city streets, on a weekday morning the traffic is minimal, and it is good to walk around, looking at the blue water, the trees that surround the water's edge, and the colorful houses perched on the hillsides that surround the reservoir. A fence surrounds the reservoir, but at places the road is within a few feet of the water. It's always peaceful to make the walk around the lake.

Usually walking around the reservoir relaxes me, but today I was keyed up and agitated. The sun reflected in the rippling water of the reservoir was beautiful, making tiny silver-colored peaks. But my mind wasn't on my surroundings. Perversely, I suppose being involved with violent death should make you more in tune with nature, but I was too preoccupied to enjoy myself.

After my walk I felt a little better. For all I knew, the police were removing a bloody sword from the apartment of one of the Yakuza while I was fretting over the taste of dishes. I decided to adopt some of the AA philosophy I've heard from Mariko and take things one day at a time, leaving things in the hands of a higher power. So I spent the rest of the day reading and resting, and tried to banish murders and mysteries and bad dreams from my mind.

When I swung by the Kawashiri Boutique to pick up Mariko that evening I was in a good mood and I had almost forgotten about Matsuda's murder or my nightmares. Mariko took me to one of the small cafes in Little Tokyo, where we enjoyed a sukiyaki dinner.

Little Tokyo has changed a lot since I've lived in Los Angeles. It used to be a quaint haven for little shops and restaurants catering to local residents. Since the effects of urban renewal it's a lot slicker, a lot more commercial, and a lot less fun.

Little Tokyo is close enough to the nest of large public buildings in downtown L.A. to be caught in urban renewal. The Otani Hotel, Japanese Village, the Golden Cherry Blossom Hotel, and Weller Court Plaza are all tangible symbols of this renewal, but change is not obtained without a price.

When the Weller Court Plaza and the new Otani Hotel were constructed in the late 1970s, several buildings, including a building known as the Sun Building, were torn down. The Sun Building had housed many old first generation Japanese, the *Issei,* and it also served as a cultural center of sorts. It was a place where *ikebana* flower-arranging lessons, Japanese folk dance clubs, and Japanese *Go* game clubs could congregate to preserve the culture and to retain some scrap of community in a rapidly changing world.

When the Sun Building and others were scheduled to be torn down to make room for the new plaza and hotel, local activists protested vehemently to the point of being arrested for disrupting the Los Angeles city council. I remember seeing my cousin Thomas, who was a protest leader, on the TV news being dragged up the aisles of the L.A. city council chamber by police. My mother, who was still alive at that time, was mortified. Now cousin Thomas sits on a couple of city commissions, and he's active in Republican politics. Time does strange things.

This disruption mirrored disruption to the community and I found it ironic that the cause of all this disruption were Japanese nationals who had decided in the 1970s that real estate in the U.S. was a good long-term investment. All this new Japanese money displaced the early Japanese pioneers that came to the U.S. to set down roots and who suffered during World War II's camps.

The place where Mariko took me for dinner was one of the few holdovers from the old Little Tokyo; it was a small storefront with booths and a mom-and-pop feel to it. As promised, Mariko paid.

"I've got another little surprise," she said at the end of dinner. "I noticed the NuArt Theater in West Los Angeles is playing one of your favorite movies."

"What's that?"

"Akira Kurosawa's *Yojimbo,* with Toshiro Mifune. It's on a double bill with *Sanjuro,* also with Mifune. *Sanjuro* is the sequel to *Yojimbo.*"

"Great," I said with genuine pleasure. "I just love *Yojimbo,* and I've never seen the sequel."

Mariko checked her watch. "We've got almost an hour to get there," she said. "So there's plenty of time."

We left the restaurant and drove my Nissan onto the Santa Monica Freeway, then onto the San Diego Freeway and off on Santa Monica Boulevard. There was the NuArt, a theater that plays a whole series of revival movies and classics.

Yojimbo ("The Bodyguard") is the story of a down-and-out samurai who comes into a town inhabited by thieves, thugs, and gamblers. The plot and staging are set in 1860 Japan, but the action and characters are taken right out of an old-fashioned American western. In fact, a Clint Eastwood western, *A Fistful of Dollars,* was later made using *Yojimbo*'s plotline.

Toshiro Mifune plays the samurai hero of the movie with a worldly, swaggering style, and his sagacity and martial skills are in sharp contrast to his grubby and disheveled appearance. I've seen *Yojimbo* three or four times, but I enjoyed it just as much this time as when I first saw it.

As do many people, I love movies. They form a common base for allusions in our society. Two hundred years ago educated people could allude to Greek myths and others would understand. A hundred years ago allusions to the Bible could be used and understood. Now it's movies.

Kurosawa movies are a special favorite of mine, and a double bill of his early samurai movies was perfect. In the second movie on the bill, *Sanjuro,* Mifune plays the same down-and-out samurai, but this time he's involved in fighting corruption within a clan. He helps a group of young boys to understand that appearances of people are not always indicators of what kind of heart and intentions they have. It reminded me of Rita Newly. In *Sanjuro,* the handsome statesman in the clan turns out to be a crook and the horse-faced administrator, the butt of caustic comments from the boys, turns out to be a capable leader interested in clearing up the corruption in the clan.

There are the typical Kurosawa twists and turns in the plot, with plenty of humor and action. The bad but handsome statesman kidnaps the good administrator, and Mifune and the boys want to rescue him. Unfortunately the boys keep dashing around like Kabuki samurai messing things up. Mifune uses his wits, skill, and experience to discover where the kidnapped administrator is being held.

After the boys have upset another of his efforts to rescue the administrator, Mifune sits with them in a hiding place scolding the boys for their foolish action and false steps, which constantly delay the resolution of the problem. 'At this rate, I'll be an old man,' the subtitle read on the screen as Mifune used his samurai sword in an effective parody of an old man with a walking stick.

After many misadventures, Mifune finally leads the boys in a successful effort to rescue the rightful head of the clan. Then, at the end, there's a tense standoff between Mifune and the chief villain. They stand facing each other for long minutes and finally engage in a quick-draw contest right out of a "B" western. Only in this movie they used swords instead of guns. Mifune, of course, wins. The boys, who witnessed the quick-draw duel, are full of admiration for Mifune. But Mifune is furious with the way the boys glorify violence. 'The best swords stay in their scabbard,' Mifune warns.

I thought about what I had seen on the screen for a long time afterward. In a way it was a kind of epiphany. But the transformation that comes with an epiphany is an emotional, not a logical, experience. And what was necessary to transform what I knew into what I could prove was logic and facts, not a sudden inspiration.

22

The next morning I called Evan Okada at the *Times*. I was almost surprised to get him personally instead of a voice mail system. Such is the pervasiveness of technology. He seemed less wary of me this time; almost friendly.

"Can you tell me some more about the Yakuza and show business?" I asked.

"Sure, what do you want to know?"

"Do you think the Yakuza would get involved in something like a burlesque theater?"

"Here, or in Japan?"

"Here."

"I doubt it. There just isn't that much money involved in something like that. The American branch of the Yakuza is involved in a few bars in Gardena and Orange County that cater to Japanese businessmen living in the area, but that's all I know of. The Yakuza involvement in show business is mostly localized to Japan."

"So they wouldn't be involved with someone like a stripper here in L.A.?"

"That would be unlikely. What do you have in mind?"

"I met a woman in Matsuda's room on the night of his murder who said she was a stripper at a local burlesque theater. I was wondering what the Yakuza's involvement might be with her."

Evan paused. "I suppose it's possible, but I still think it's unlikely. There are a lot of Yakuza in Hawaii, but they aren't that active here in California yet. I can't imagine they would get involved in penny-ante stuff like a burlesque theater. They all seem to have bigger fish to fry."

I sighed. "Okay. So much for that idea."

"What idea?"

Evan's reporter's instincts were aroused.

"I just had a notion about Matsuda's murder. Both the Yakuza and the Americans arrested the other day denied they killed Matsuda, and I had an idea about the killing."

"Which was?"

A leading question. Evan was in full reporter mode now. "Which was something that probably won't pan out. It was more in the nature of a hunch instead of a real idea. I'll tell you what, if something comes of it I'll make you a deal."

"What kind of deal?"

"If I come up with anything, I'll call you. It may or may not be something interesting to you, but you can decide for yourself."

"Now you've got my curiosity piqued," Evan said.

"Don't be too curious. It probably won't pan out. If it does pan out, I'll contact you."

I hung up and got dressed. I went down to the office and started working again on the L.A. Mystery Club plot. I wrote my newly acquired samurai sword into the mystery's plotline, but I had a hard time concentrating. My concocted mystery seemed contrived and too neatly packaged. It didn't have the puzzling ambiguities that characterize real life. If it did, I'd get (and deserve) a torrent of complaints about all the loose ends from the people trying to solve the mystery. People don't want to spend all day chasing around Los Angeles only to be told there isn't an answer to some pieces of the puzzle.

In the afternoon I called Lieutenant Johnson to see if he had uncovered any evidence that the Yakuza or Rita were guilty of Matsuda's death. He seemed surprised that I called him and told me in a professionally brisk manner that the LAPD didn't discuss ongoing investigations.

"Look, maybe there is something you can tell me."

"I just told you I can't give out information on an ongoing investigation, Mr. Tanaka. We appreciate your help on this matter, but you really should leave this to the professionals."

"It's not really about the investigation," I said hastily. "It's actually about something that happened fifty years ago. You've got records of Matsuda's past, don't you?"

"Yes." A very cautious tone, but it wasn't exasperated yet. I hurried forward with my request.

"The *Times* article said he left the United States right after the war and renounced his citizenship."

"That's right."

"Can you tell me if Matsuda was in a relocation camp during the war, and if so, which one?"

A slight pause, then Johnson said, "I suppose so, if that's all you want to know. Wait a minute while I look at my file on Matsuda." There was a several-minute pause while my excitement started growing. Finally, Johnson came back on the line and said, "Matsuda was in the Heart Mountain relocation camp for the duration of the war. Does that mean anything to you?"

I sighed. "No, it doesn't. I just had a hunch that didn't pan out. Thanks for your help." I was sure that Matsuda would have been in Manzanar. Heart Mountain threw me for a loop. More frustration.

That left the woman I saw in Matsuda's room as the only key I had left to unraveling his murder. I could think of one contact that might be able to help me find her, but I wasn't sure if her boyfriend really knew where she was anyway. Besides, one encounter with him was enough. I thought of another contact that might be able to help, but didn't want to pursue that either. Then I finally thought of a third.

Mariko had another AA meeting that night, this time a discussion group on the twelve steps, not one where she would talk. She called me at the office as the boutique was closing to see how I was feeling (still sore) and to remind me she had a meeting. "What are you going to do tonight?" she asked.

"I'm going to see a stripper."

A long pause. "And . . ."

"And, indeed. I don't know. I want to talk to her. I intend to see her after she's done her act, so I'll be out late. I'll see you to-morrow and fill you in on the details."

I killed a few hours after dinner at my apartment watching TV, but I was anxious to get going and left my house way too early. I drove to the Paradise Vineyard and pulled into the alley behind it. I parked about two hundred feet from the stage door. A weak light illuminated the alley by the door. I waited.

I hoped my second stakeout would be more successful than my first, but despite my excitement I still found it incredibly boring work. It was sort of like fishing, however, in that any little nibble freshened your interest until you realized it wasn't the fish you were waiting for.

I saw several men walk in through the stage door. Most of them left with women. But I didn't see the particular person I was look-ing for. Finally, at around midnight, I saw her come out. She was with a surprisingly well-dressed older man. She was hanging onto his arm and laughing.

I got out of the car and walked over to the couple. At the sight of a stranger approaching them in the alley, they slowed down and watched me warily. At past midnight in a back alley in downtown Los Angeles, it isn't a good practice to go along blindly when you see a stranger.

"Ms. Martinez?" I called out.

The redheaded Latina recognized me and said something to her companion. He hung back reluctantly, almost as if he didn't want me to see his face.

Rosie Martinez walked forward to meet me. "What the hell do you want?" she said.

"Well, hello to you, too."

She looked over her shoulder at her companion. "Look, my gentleman friend is crapping in his pants. He's afraid we'll get busted, because I told him you were a cop."

"I'm not a cop. I told you that before."

"Well, what do ya want?" she asked.

"I want to talk to Angela Sanchez."

"Shit, I told you I don't know where she is. Talk to Fred about that."

"I talked to Fred and he said he didn't know where she is. I think he's lying. I'm not trying to be offensive, Ms. Martinez, but I think you're lying, too."

"What the hell . . ."

"Please don't get mad at me. Believe it or not, I really want to help Angela. She can help me and I can help her. She doesn't have to hide. The police caught the two guys that Matsuda was working for."

"Who's Matsuda?"

"The guy who was killed at the hotel. The guy Angela was with that night. She doesn't have to be afraid of them and she doesn't have to be afraid of me. Believe me, you'll be helping her by telling me where she is. I really do want to help her, and I think I can."

Martinez looked at me in the half-light of the alley. "You look like shit," she said.

"I got beat up," I said, shrugging. "The two guys who did it were the two guys who were arrested. The same guys Matsuda was working for."

"They're in the can?"

"That's right."

"I still don't know nothin' about Angela."

"Okay, I'll come clean with you. I'm trying to collect a reward put up by a Japanese business association. If I can prove my involvement in the case, they'll pay me the money, but now they're questioning if I met Matsuda before he was murdered and they're trying to wriggle out of giving me the cash. Angela can back up my story. I didn't want to tell you about it because I didn't want to share it with her. I'm sorry about that, but I guess I'm willing to split it with her if she'll back me up about meeting Matsuda."

My lie didn't even make real sense to me, but the part about money and businessmen trying to wriggle out of payment seemed to make sense to Martinez.

"How much money?" she asked.

This put me in a little dilemma. If I said an amount too large, she would catch on to my lie, but if I said something too small, she might not be interested in spilling what she knew. I picked a figure. "Ten thousand dollars. If Angela backs me up, I'll give her a thousand."

"Two thousand, and I get something, too." She had the heart of an agent.

"Fifteen hundred, and anything you get is between Angela and you." Maybe I should have just said okay, but my instincts told me she'd expect me to bargain.

She made a quick decision, the kind of decision people make when they're street smart and used to living by their wits. "Okay. She's at the Blue Surf Motel in Long Beach. Room 212. She had me bring some stuff down to her. I'm going to tell her about the fifteen hundred, so don't try to stiff her."

"All right, Ms. Martinez. Thank you. I appreciate it."

She nodded slowly and turned back to go with her companion, reassuring him that everything was going to be okay, that he wasn't going to be busted, compromised, or blackmailed.

23

The Blue Surf Motel is an old stucco structure off Pacific Coast Highway in north Long Beach. In that section of Long Beach, Pacific Coast Highway is nowhere near the Pacific Coast. It's miles from the beach as it makes its way toward an infamous traffic circle with a history of so many accidents that I'm convinced it was designed to reduce California's surplus population. Local legend says the designer of the traffic circle died there in a car accident, but I think this is just an urban legend that was created to inject some justice in the universe.

The pink stucco of the building was chipped, showing white plaster underneath, and I was surprised to see the U-shaped motel was only one-story high. Since I had been told that Angela Sanchez was in room 212, I had expected to find a two-story building. Driving into the U-shaped motel court, I found that the rooms to my left were numbered in the one hundreds, the rooms to my right were in the three hundreds, and the rooms at the far end of the U were numbered in the two hundreds.

I parked my car by the door to room 212, and walked up to it. Inside I could hear the TV. A game show. I knocked, and the volume of the TV was turned down. I knocked a second time.

"Who's there?"

"My name is Ken Tanaka."

A pause. "I don't know you."

"As a matter of fact, I think you do. I believe we met once, Ms. Sanchez."

"How the hell did you find me?"

"A friend of yours told me."

"Fred?"

"No, someone else."

The door opened a crack. The safety chain was on. Through the narrow opening, I saw a three-inch strip of her face, and red hair. One eye peered through the opening of the door. "It's you!" she said with surprise.

"That's right. I told you we met once."

"Are you the one with the reward?"

"I'd like to talk to you about that. Can I come in?"

Silence. Her eye continued to study me. I couldn't get a reading on the expression on the rest of her face. Finally, "What the hell happened to your face?"

"I got beat up. You should have seen it before the swelling started going down. Two guys that Matsuda worked with did the beating. But now they're in jail. That's one of the reasons they're in jail and one of the reasons I helped put them in. Now I think I can help you. Can I come in? I'd really like to talk to you."

The eye studied me for a few more seconds, then the door closed. I could hear the safety chain rattling. The door opened once again. "Come in," she said.

I walked into a crowded motel room. Three suitcases were piled in a corner. The bed was messed up where she had been lying watching TV. An open, half eaten two-pound box of See's Candies lay on the bed. On the wall was a painting of a sunset done in oranges, reds, and whites. It was a boat on the water. It looked like the sort of thing that's painted by machines.

"There's no chair," she said. "Sit down." She pointed at the bed. On her hands she was still wearing the multitude of rings.

I sat down gingerly on the edge of the bed, and so did she.

"What the hell do ya want?" she asked.

"I want to talk about the night you were with Matsuda. I even went to your apartment and tried to talk to your boyfriend."

"Armondo. He's an asshole. He acts like Mr. *Macho,* but he ain't worth shit. That's why I dumped him and hid out here. What's this about a reward?"

Her boyfriend seemed plenty tough to me, but I wasn't going to argue the point. Besides, it was time to 'fess up.

"There actually isn't a reward. I just had to talk to you, and Ms. Martinez wasn't going to tell me where you were without some reason other than my wanting it."

She gave me a look that said that being lied to by a man was pretty much what she expected. It made me feel crummy. I tried a different tack. "What's got you so scared?"

"Shit. You heard 'bout what they did to that guy?" she said.

"I heard about what somebody did to Matsuda."

"I'm next."

"Who told you that?"

No answer.

"Look, there's no reason for you to be scared, and there's no reason for you to hide. The police want to talk to you, but not as a suspect in the murder of Matsuda, just to hear your story of what went on that night. I've got an interest because I want you to confirm that I was in and out of his hotel room. The police don't suspect me in the murder anymore, and I don't think they ever suspected you."

"The cops ain't the only ones I'm worried about."

"If you're worried about the Yakuza, the Japanese Mafia, I told you the two guys that Matsuda worked for are already in jail. You don't have anything to fear. They weren't after you, anyway."

"That's not what I was told."

"By who?"

More silence. She stared at me, her face not giving away her emotions. Finally she said, "Fred Yoshida."

"I know that Fred is very good to you. He probably helped you with your act and your dancing. But he's got his own interests in this affair, and what he has to hide has nothing to do with you."

"He told me they're out to get me," she said all at once. "It's some kind of Japanese thing. They'll cut me like they cut that guy up. Fred said the only way to save my ass is to stay here and then move out of town. He even paid for this room, and he said he'll help me scrape up enough money to move."

"What happened that night?"

"When that guy was killed?"

"That's right."

"I don't know. I really don't. But Fred said they thought I knew and that's why the Japanese Mafia is after me."

"Fred lied to you."

She received this assertion in silence. I tried again. "After I left you that night, what happened?"

She gave a half smile. "Ya want all the dirty details?"

I smiled back and shook my head. "No, I mean after you and Matsuda were done. What happened?"

She shrugged. "We went to the Paradise. Matsuda picked me up in a bar between shows. I like to turn a trick when I can," she said matter-of-factly. "Japanese businessmen are always good Johns; they're clean, not often kinky, and good tippers."

"So Matsuda didn't know that you worked at the Paradise Vineyard?"

"No. Like I said, he met me in a bar. After we were done, I told him to come to the theater to see the show. I thought he'd be a good John to keep in touch with, because he said he came to L.A. a lot. It doesn't hurt to have a regular bunch of tricks. He came backstage with me and saw Fred. He just about shit. He said they hadn't seen each other for fifty years. They said they were in some kind of concentration camp together during World War Two."

"And?"

"And then I did my act. The next day some guy from the cops shows up at the theater wanting to know who was with Matsuda the night before. I was scared and didn't say nothin', so he said he'd be back with someone who could identify me. I suppose that was you."

I nodded.

"Fred came after me and told me to get out, that it ain't just the cops looking for me, that this Japanese Mafia wanted me, too. He told me Matsuda was cut to pieces, and it scared the piss out of me. He helped me get this room, and he's been helping me pay for it. I've been bored here, but scared shitless to leave until Fred told me it was safe."

I nodded. "I think it's safe, now."

I drove back to L.A. feeling pretty good about linking Yoshida and Matsuda, even if it was fifty years ago. Matsuda being in Heart Mountain and Yoshida being in Manzanar puzzled me, but Angela said they had told her they were in a camp together, so there had to be some connection. I didn't quite know what that meant yet. Before I would turn my information over to Lieutenant Johnson I decided to try and package things up neatly with documentation, and I knew just where to go for that.

About a block from the Kawashiri Boutique is the Japanese American National Museum, near Alameda and First Street. I was in it when it first opened, but I'm embarrassed to say that I was in it only once. When I had been there for the opening, something caught my eye, and when I talked to Mrs. Okada she reminded me of it. In the basement of the museum is an entire room devoted to the relocation camps. In this room is a computer system set up so you can search for the camp record of any inmate.

When I got to the museum I assuaged my conscience by paying the modest membership fee and joining the museum. Then, after asking the staff at the reception desk if the camp computer was still in the basement, I took the elevator down. The computer was a simple PC, and it took me only a few seconds to figure out how to use the database.

When I did an inquiry on Fred Yoshida in Manzanar, the system came back with the message:

No record for Fred Yoshida at Manzanar.

Just what I expected. I still didn't know exactly what to make of the lie, but Angela said that Yoshida and Matsuda were in camp together, which meant Yoshida had to be in Heart Mountain Camp. I did a screen printout to show that Fred Yoshida had no record for Manzanar.

Then I did an inquiry for Susumu Matsuda in Heart Mountain Camp. Matsuda's camp record came up. I did a printout of that.

Then I did an inquiry for Fred Yoshida in Heart Mountain. To my surprise I got the message:

No record for Fred Yoshida at Heart Mountain.

Like anyone else, I tried the inquiry a second time. Naturally, I got the same result.

I was stumped. I wanted to tear into the guts of the program to see if there was some programming error, but obviously the museum wasn't going to let a visitor do that. Instead, I printed out a list of all the Yoshida's at Heart Mountain to see if I could see a "Frederick" or something similar instead of "Fred." Yoshida's a common name, so there were several names on the list, but none that looked like Fred. Could Yoshida have lied about being in camp? If so, why had he and Matsuda told Angela that they knew each other from camp?

On an impulse, I tried Naomi Okada at Heart Mountain. I got the message:

No record for Naomi Okada at Heart Mountain.

There had to be a problem. Mrs. Okada told me that she not only looked up her records on the museum computer, she was even able to get her camp files from the National Archives. I knew she had been at Heart Mountain. I considered the possibility that the programmer who put together the system made some kind of programming mistake. Then the answer dawned on me. It was so simple I almost hit myself in the head. Maybe I wasn't really cut out for a career in detecting or in computers.

I did a printout of the Yoshidas at Manzanar to make sure. As with Heart Mountain, there were no "Fred" or "Frederick" Yoshidas listed, but there were several Yoshidas, just as there would be several "Smith" or "Jones" listings in a phone book. If I could get to the program I could do the next step automatically, but instead I took the printouts with me back to the office to do things the old-fashioned way, by hand.

When I was at the museum I learned that Heart Mountain had fewer than twelve thousand inmates, which made it like a small town. In small towns everyone knows everyone's business, and I had talked to a friendly resident of Heart Mountain only a few days before. I picked up the phone and called Mrs. Okada.

She was surprised to hear from me again and doubly surprised to hear I wanted to talk to her and not her grandson. She was almost astounded when I said I wanted to talk some more about Heart Mountain Camp. She agreed to see me immediately.

When I reached her house, we again went through the little dance over tea. It's sort of a modern Japanese tea ceremony. Finally we settled in to talk.

"Well, I appreciate your taking the time to talk to me."

"Are you writing a book about life at Heart Mountain?"

"Actually, I'm interested in one of the people in the camp at the time you were there."

"Who?"

"A Mr. Susumu Matsuda."

"Oh," Mrs. Okada said, surprised. "Is that what you're here about?"

"What do you mean?"

"I mean about the murder in the camp."

"Mr. Matsuda was involved in a murder?"

"Well, indirectly," she said. "It was his girlfriend, Yuki Yoshida, who was killed."

Like I said, Yoshida is a common Japanese name, but I took a chance. "Did Yuki Yoshida have a brother or a relative who wanted to be a dancer?"

"Of course! Jiro, her brother. We used to call him Fred, because he always wanted to be Fred Astaire. He was always involved in some kind of show or entertainment."

"And his sister was killed?"

Mrs. Okada shook her head. "Yes, it was a terrible thing. She went out one night, and they found her body the next morning."

"What happened?"

"She went out after curfew. Sneaking out was something we did, usually to meet boys." A wisp of a smile crossed her face. "Or just for the fun of it. Anyway, poor Yuki must have been attacked. Her skull was crushed by a rock. They found her body the next morning. They did an investigation, but I think it was one of the white guards that did it, and they did a cover-up because of that."

"And Jiro, Fred, was her brother?"

"That's right. He wasn't at the camp at the time. He had volunteered for the army. He was a yes-yes man."

"What's that mean?"

"Oh, in the camps the government wanted us to sign a complicated loyalty oath. For the men, two of the questions on it asked if they would fight for the United States and if they gave up any allegiance to a foreign power. That meant Japan. A lot of the men didn't like these questions. A huge number were U.S. citizens who thought of themselves as loyal Americans, and they thought it was an insult to say they ever had any allegiance to any country but the U.S. Others felt it was unfair for the U.S. to ask if they would fight when their families were being held in the camps."

"And Fred Yoshida answered 'yes' to both questions?"

"That's right. That's why he was a yes-yes man. Most men answered yes-yes. I can't remember the exact number, but I think it was something like eighty-five percent said they would fight for the U.S. even though we were in the camps."

"And that's how they formed the Four Forty-second and other Nisei combat units?"

She nodded.

"The Four Forty-second had a great record."

"That's because they used those boys for cannon fodder," she said. "It was terrible. They wouldn't complain in public, but a lot of them wrote home that they were always being put in the heavy fighting because the generals didn't want to use white troops. They felt they had to endure it or else people would say they were disloyal to the U.S."

"I knew about the Four Forty-second record, but it never occurred to me why they earned so many medals, citations, and Purple Hearts for a unit their size. I suppose that when Fred Yoshida answered yes to both questions, he joined the army."

"That's right," she said. "But something happened to him. I can't remember if he was hurt in combat or something. Anyway, he was in a hospital when Yuki was killed. He couldn't even go to her funeral."

"He was hurt in a training accident with a hand grenade."

She looked surprised. "How did you know that?"

"He told me."

"You've talked to him?"

"Yes."

"Oh," she said. "Is he still working at that place?" She said the last two words with a clear tone of disapproval.

"Yes, he is."

She snorted in disgust. "He claims that's the only kind of job he can get where he's involved in show business and in choreographing dancing. If that's the case he should get a job where he isn't involved in show business or dancing."

I shrugged. "Could you tell me more about Mr. Matsuda?"

"Susumu was a no-no man and a *kibei*."

"Kibei? That's a word I'm not familiar with."

"A kibei was someone who was educated in Japan, even though he was an American. Most of us were educated in the U.S. and bought into the American dream. But since they were educated in Japan, the kibeis had a hard time adjusting, and I think that was one reason Susumu answered 'no' to both questions about renouncing allegiance and being willing to fight for the U.S. After the war he actually emigrated to Japan and even gave up his U.S. citizenship. It was a big scandal. I've never thought about it before, but his first name, Susumu, means 'to go forward' in Japanese. Yet he was someone who always wanted to go back."

"What kind of person was he?"

"He took being sent to the camps personally." She paused. "I guess it was personal. But it wasn't because of anything we had done as individuals; it was because of us being Japanese. The Germans and Italians weren't put in camps, just us. Susumu just rebelled about the whole notion of being in camp and said it really didn't prove our loyalty if we cooperated. So he was always getting into some kind of trouble."

"What kind of trouble?"

"Little things. There were all these rumors that he was involved in some kind of theft with the gangs in the camp, but Yuki said it wasn't true, and I guess she would know."

"And she was Matsuda's girlfriend?"

"At least until the incident of the yes-yes and no-no questions came up. In fact, people my age still have hard feelings about the whole yes-yes and no-no controversy. It sounds silly, but there are still fights about this, even after all these years. People still hate each other because they were on one side of the issue or the other. It's strange. It should all be history now, but instead it still seems that the feelings are strong and fresh as ever. Yuki sided with her brother at the time. Fred said the only way to prove that we were really loyal was to say yes-yes to both questions and to fight for the United States. Susumu and Fred had a big fight over that. That sort of broke up Yuki and Susumu, too."

"And then Yuki got murdered?"

"Yes, about two months after the fight. After Fred had gone off to the army and got hurt."

"And you think one of the guards killed her?"

"They had a big investigation, but it was all a phony thing. They never came up with any suspects. It was just a cover-up. It was disgusting."

"By the way, Mrs. Okada, Okada is your married name, isn't it?" I asked.

"Yes. My maiden name was Hirao."

"So your camp records would be listed under Hirao?"

"Yes, Naomi Hirao."

"Just as Fred Yoshida's records would be listed under Jiro Yoshida. Both of you have your camp records listed under names that you don't use now." That's why I couldn't find their records when I did my search. I silently apologized to the programmer who set up the museum's system for suspecting there was a bug.

"Did Fred return to Heart Mountain after his injury?" I continued.

"No. They thought there might be trouble because a guard probably killed his sister. So they shipped poor Fred and his entire family off to Manzanar. They were always shuffling people around from camp to camp to separate who they thought might be troublemakers." She brightened up a bit. "Are you investigating Yuki's murder? That happened fifty years ago."

"No, I'm not investigating Yuki Yoshida's murder," I said. "I'm investigating Susumu Matsuda's murder. Didn't you see the article about him in the *L.A. Times?*"

"I told you that with my eyes I can't read too much anymore. I knew about the murder in Little Tokyo, but I didn't know that was the same Matsuda who was at Heart Mountain with me." She shook her head. "Well, it's a small world, isn't it?"

The backstage of the Paradise Vineyard had the same spooky feeling that I felt every time I walked in there. I supposed that after awhile you'd get used to being backstage. But as a novice not quite understanding the workings of the theater, I still found it surprising and disquieting to see behind the magic that I usually saw when facing a stage.

Nobody challenged me as I walked through the stage door and made my way back to the practice area, where I saw Yoshida sitting at a table doing some paperwork. On his lap sat his cane.

"Hello," I said.

Yoshida looked up from his writing. "Hello."

"I came back to talk to you again."

"I can see that."

I looked around for a chair to sit on. Not seeing one handy, I stood. "I saw a mutual friend of ours this morning."

"Who's that?"

"Angela Sanchez. She says that on the night that Matsuda was killed, he came back with her to the theater, where he met you. She said that you two knew each other, but you hadn't seen each other for fifty years."

"Yes, that's true," he said. "We almost didn't recognize each other."

"I can imagine. Fifty years is a long time."

"A very long time."

"But evidently not long enough to forgive some things."

"What do you mean?"

"I'm not quite sure, but I think I have most things figured out. About Matsuda's murder, I mean. But not the motive."

"What are you talking about?"

"I think we both know what I'm talking about."

"You think I was involved in Matsuda's murder? Just because we knew each other? That night was the first time we met in fifty years. I didn't mention it to the police because I didn't want to get involved."

"Is not getting involved why you paid for Angela's motel room in Long Beach? You told her to get out of town, that the Yakuza was after her."

"I didn't tell her that."

"She says you did. She really likes and respects you. She trusts you. It's a shame you used that trust against her."

"Just what do you mean?"

"Like I said, I think I have most things figured out. That night Matsuda met Angela in the bar. She turned a trick with him and then invited him to come back to the theater to see her act. I guess she is a very friendly girl, or maybe Matsuda was a big tipper. Who knows. For whatever reason, he came back with her, probably because the little piece of business he had to do with me had been completed.

"Anyway, he was very surprised to see someone he hadn't seen for fifty years when he walked backstage. That was you, the brother of the woman he used to date. You see, I found out that you were in Heart Mountain Camp before you were in Manzanar. I even have your records of when you were at Heart Mountain and when you were at Manzanar. I was able to match your name on two lists to make sure the same Jiro Yoshida was in two camps. I even learned that Matsuda and Yuki were boyfriend and girlfriend when they were in the camps, before the big blowup over the loyalty oath occurred."

Yoshida looked surprised, but made no comment.

"Anyway, he came back here and met you. Then I think you two guys went out for a drink, maybe at the same bar you took me to. It would probably be easy enough to check with the bartender to find out for sure.

"Afterward, you and Matsuda went back to his room and something happened there. Something happened that was so horrendous it made you lose all control, and you took out the sword hidden in the cane that you carry."

I saw Yoshida's hand tightening around the shaft of his cane, and I knew my guess was right. I thanked Kurosawa and the sword/cane scene in *Sanjuro*. "Then you hacked Matsuda to pieces. When you were done, you put on your overcoat, which covered most of the bloodstains on your clothing, and left his room."

"You're pretty good," Yoshida said. "Maybe it's because you're smart. Japanese tend to be smart."

"That's as much a racial stereotype as the one that says we're inscrutable and that we can't show emotion. You and I both know that we can show a lot of emotion. In fact, Japanese view themselves as very emotional people. Because of that emotion, we get in trouble a lot. Like when you lost your temper and killed Matsuda. The one thing I don't know is what caused it. I think the police can prove everything else, but they'll never know the cause unless you tell them.

"Angela will testify that you and Matsuda met here at the theater. I know someone who was in the Heart Mountain Relocation Camp with you who will testify that she knew Matsuda when he used to date your sister, Yuki. If you and Matsuda didn't go to the same bar that we did, then it must be another one around here locally. I'm sure the police will be able to find out from the bartender that you two guys were in drinking on the night Matsuda was killed.

"That sword cane of yours is a pretty good idea for someone who has to work late in downtown L.A. But no matter how carefully you've cleaned the blade, there will be some microscopic bloodstains still on it that the police will be able to find. In any case, the inside of one of your coats will have bloodstains that the police will be able to match to Matsuda's. But like I said, the one thing that's missing is why you did it. Originally I thought this had something to do with the Yakuza, but although Matsuda was involved with the Yakuza, I don't think you are. There's another reason. A reason so bad that you got into a rage and hacked him to pieces."

"He killed my sister," Yoshida said simply.

"Yuki?"

"Yes."

"I thought she was murdered by one of the camp guards?"

"So did I. For fifty years. But I guess seeing me after all these years shocked Susumu. After we went drinking together he got very drunk and admitted that he killed Yuki. He started crying. In his room he begged for forgiveness. He got on his knees and bowed in an old-fashioned kowtow right there on the floor until his forehead hit the ground, begging for forgiveness.

"He said he still loved Yuki after the big fight over the loyalty oath, but that Yuki didn't want to have much to do with him because of the fight between him and me. He said that he wanted to reconcile with Yuki, and on the night she was murdered they met so they could talk with each other. He told her he wanted to go back to Japan after the war, no matter who won. He wanted her to come with him.

"She got mad at him. For some reason she got it into her head that maybe he'd come round to my way of thinking, and she was expecting him to tell her that he was going to volunteer for the army and fight for the U.S. Since I was in a hospital after my accident, Yuki felt strong feelings of patriotism, and she was upset with Matsuda when he said that he hated the U.S. and wanted to go back to Japan. He said he got so mad at her that he pushed her down and she hit her head on a rock. He said it was an accident. I don't know if that was true or not. It didn't make any difference to me.

"For half a century I thought one of the white guards had killed my sister. That was the icing on the cake for everything else that white society had done to me. Here in this country my ambitions, my life, what I could and could not do, where I could and could not go, all those things were restricted because I had a yellow face in a white society. The fact that we were in the camps in the first place was because we were Japanese in a white man's world in the United States.

"When I got torn up by the hand grenade, it was because some meathead sergeant, who probably couldn't even read and write, was put in charge of training Japanese troops. It was probably punishment for him because he wasn't good enough to train white troops.

"I was lying in the hospital torn up in pain, knowing that whatever slim chance I might ever have of making it as a song and dance man in this society had disappeared in a shower of smoke and shell fragments. Then I heard that my only sister had been killed. I was told that it was by one of the white guards and that they had involved themselves in a cover-up to protect the real murderer. For fifty years that hate had been added on top of all the others and it stayed locked up in here." He struck his chest.

"Then Matsuda told me that he was the one who killed my sister. The lousy kibei who wanted to go back to Japan, who didn't want to stay in white society and fight it out and try to do something despite the obstacles that we had. He killed my sister just because she got mad at him and had a fight with him about going back to Japan."

Yoshida looked up at me. His eyes looked very tired. "Something inside me just snapped then. I took out my sword from my cane." He grasped the top of his cane with one hand and the shaft with the other and pulled them apart a few inches, showing me the gleaming sword blade held in the cane. "And I started hitting him and hitting him with the sword, hacking him to pieces. I just couldn't stop." Yoshida started crying.

"Why did he tell you he killed your sister?" I asked. "I mean, after fifty years, why didn't he just keep his mouth shut?"

"You're Japanese," Yoshida said. "You should know that Japanese have a compulsion to apologize, sometimes even when they haven't done anything wrong. Remember when they had that big cyclamate scare, when they said that cyclamates in soft drinks cause cancer?"

"Yes."

"Well, in Japan when they took the cyclamates out of the soft drinks, all the Japanese soft drink companies published big ads apologizing to the public for putting something which might be unhealthful into their drinks. What was funny about that was that companies that never used cyclamates in their soft drinks also published apologies. They apologized because they *might* have used something unhealthy in their drinks, even though they didn't. Typically Japanese. Don't you sometimes apologize when you've never really done anything?"

"I've never thought about it, but I guess that's true," I said.

"It's part of the social legacy we Japanese have along with the exaggerated politeness and the stiff social customs between strangers. When Matsuda got drunk, his defenses went down. I guess the shock of seeing me after all those years set him off, asking for forgiveness for Yuki's murder, although he called it an accident. For all I know, it *was* an accident. I guess it doesn't make any difference now."

"No, I guess it doesn't," I said. "I'm going to have to call the police."

"I know. Weren't you afraid I'd do something to you when you came here?"

"No. You had some reason for what you did to Matsuda. I didn't think you'd have the same kind of rage against me. In addition to the police, I think we should also call a lawyer. If you don't have one, I can recommend a good one. He's the cousin of my girlfriend."

"*Shigata ga nai,*" he said. "I guess it doesn't matter to me one way or the other."

"Then, I'll call you a lawyer. You'll need one. Can I ask you something?"

"What?"

"Why did you tell me all this? I mean about why you did it to Matsuda."

Yoshida looked up at me, an expression of ineffable sadness in his eyes. "I told you, we Japanese have a compulsion to apologize. I was sorry."

26

The office door opened and a timid soul stuck his head in. Mariko was sitting in front of a typing stand with an old-fashioned manual typewriter on it, buffing her nails. She looked smashing in a silk jade-colored top and a long black leather skirt that was slit to the thigh.

" 'Nother customer, Boss!" she said, popping the gum she was chewing. "C'mon in," she said.

The newcomer entered the office and tentatively made his way toward my desk.

"Am I in the right place?" he asked.

I pushed my hat back on my head and leaned back in my chair. "I don't know," I answered. "Where do you want to be?"

"I'm new at this, and I want to make sure I'm at the right place."

A newbie, I thought; someone new to mystery weekends. I broke character for a moment and said, "If you're participating in the L.A. Mystery Club's mystery weekend, you're in the right place."

"Oh good. I'm, ah . . ."

"Are you looking for someone?" I coaxed.

"Yes. A Mr. Ken Tanaka, Private Detective."

"I'm Tanaka. What do you want?"

"Ah, I guess I'm supposed to ask for more information."

"What kind of information?"

He shrugged. "I don't really know."

"Well, have you stopped by the Kawashiri Boutique to talk to Big Mama Kawashiri?"

"Is that on the map they gave me when I registered for the event?"

"Yep. If you go and talk to Big Mama you might find out some things that will help you when you come back here to ask for more information."

"Okay, thanks," he said as he started backing out of the office.

"Psst!" Mariko beckoned him in a loud stage whisper.

He looked a little startled and walked over to her. I started looking down at some paperwork on the desk as Mariko gave an exaggerated glance in my direction. She then reached into the top of her blouse and withdrew a folded slip of paper. "Take this and read it before you talk to Big Mama! Tell her you've come to talk to her about the Jade Penguin. But for God's sake be careful and don't read the note until you leave the office!"

"Ah, thank you," the newbie said, stuffing the note into his pocket.

When he left, Mariko gave me a big grin and patted her chest. "I'm going to have to prepare some more notes to stuff in here," she said. "I think I'm down to around five. We're getting a lot more people playing today than we expected."

"That's great," I answered.

The door opened again, and Ezekiel and Mary Maloney entered together.

"A couple of people we've seen before, Boss," Mariko said.

"Relax," Mary said, "This is a social call. We just stopped by to see how it's going and to see if you needed a soft drink or something like that."

"It's going pretty good, and we packed our own lunches and snacks, thank you. Have you already solved it?" I asked.

"Heck, no," Mary said. "I certainly wouldn't travel with the likes of Ezekiel if I was out hunting clues. He's likely to benefit from my superior investigative skills. We just decided to take a short break and see if you needed anything."

Ezekiel snorted a reply, but made no comment. I was sure Mary was the one who thought to see if we needed anything, but I appreciated Ezekiel tagging along.

"Everything okay?" Ezekiel asked.

"I just asked that," Mary said.

"I mean with the real case."

"I guess so. I'll have to testify, but the wheels of real justice turn exceedingly slow. It's not like our mystery weekends where everything is neatly solved by the awards banquet at 7:30 P.M."

"Well, I'm sure that today more than a few people are just going to write down guesses by the time the deadline approaches to name the murderer. You did a good job."

"Thanks."

"By the way," Mary said casually, "I've found that Kendo is not only the name of your detective agency, it's also the word for Japanese fencing. I suppose that unusual Japanese sword at the murder scene has something to do with that link, huh?"

I grinned. "That's the oldest one in the book, Mary, and I'm surprised you tried it on me. You won't pick up any clues from me by watching my reactions to your statements."

Mary grinned back, "Well it was worth a try. Ezekiel suggested I try it, anyway."

From the look on Ezekiel's face, I could tell her statement was true and started laughing.

"No hint intended, but where did you pick up that sword?" she asked.

"I got it at a garage sale. The woman who sold it to me said her late husband picked it up in Japan, right after the war."

"That's an unusual pattern on the blade."

"Yeah, after this weekend's over I'm going to see if I can do some research to see if I can find out more about the sword."

"We have to go," Ezekiel said abruptly. "I want to find more clues."

Mary gave a shrug and blew me and Mariko a kiss. She and Ezekiel left. Ezekiel didn't bother to say good-bye.

Mariko was about to say something to me when another person stuck her head into the office. She immediately got into character, and sang out, "Looks like another new client, Boss!"

The new player was a short woman with frizzy black hair. She came into the office and approached my desk.

"Are you Ken Tanaka, Private Detective?"

I liked the sound of that. I sat back in my chair and said, "Yes, I am."